D0253473

ALSO KNOWN AS
ROWAN POHI

ALSO KNOWN AS
ROWAN POHI

RALPH FLETCHER

GRAPHIA

HOUGHTON MIFFLIN HARCOURT / BOSTON NEW YORK

www.hmhbooks.com

The text of this book is set in Phontina MT.
Book design by Sharismar Rodriguez

The Library of Congress has cataloged the hardcover edition as follows:
Fletcher, Ralph J.
Also known as Rowan Pohi / Ralph Fletcher.
p. cm.
Summary: After impulsively lying his way into an elite preparatory school,
sophomore Bobby Steele hopes to escape the shame of his father's well-publicized
incarceration but keeps waiting for his secret to be revealed.

[1. Identity—Fiction. 2. Family problems—Fiction. 3. High schools—Fiction.
4. Schools—Fiction. 5. Brothers—Fiction. 6. Social class—Fiction.] I. Title.

PZ7.F632115Als 2011
[Fic]—dc22   2011009641

ISBN: 978-0-547-57208-6 hardcover
ISBN: 978-0-547-85154-9 paperback

Manufactured in the United States of America
DOC 10 9 8 7 6 5 4 3 2 1
4500394404

For Chris Crutcher
fine writer and friend
who helped me envision this book
when it was still a tiny wet thing,
rising from the straw on wobbly legs

ONE

IT WAS BIG POOBS WHO FIRST SUGGESTED THE IDEA. WE were at the International House of Pancakes: Poobs, Marcus, and me. The tables at the IHOP are sometimes sticky with syrup, but it's the only place around where a kid can order a coffee or soda and nobody complains if he wants to hang out for an hour or two.

The booths were crowded, mostly with Whitestone Prep kids. Stonys, we called them. Even without their green uniform shirts, they were obviously Stonys. They were the ones with braces and designer jeans. The ones with new backpacks. The ones talking about "wild times" at summer music camp in places like Tanglewood or Chautauqua.

Five Stony girls were jammed into the booth next to us. The tallest girl was blond and cute; very. They were talking about college. I heard her say something about coed dorms, which made the other girls giggle.

Marcus spun his fork like he was playing spin-the-bottle, except there was no girl in his near future, and no college either. After (more like *if*) he graduated from Riverview High, he was joining the Marines.

The three of us leaned back in our seats. We were beyond bored.

Big Poobs sighed. "Let's do something."

Poobs was a straight-C student, except for the occasional D. There was no college in his plans either, but he didn't need it any more than Marcus did. His parents owned Vinny's, a popular local Italian restaurant. Big Poobs worked busing tables there. In a year he would be a waiter; eventually he would own the restaurant himself.

My grades were actually good, but with Mom gone for over a year now, and no sign of her coming back, I couldn't picture myself waltzing off to the University of Whatever after high school. I figured I should stick around for my little brother, Cody, at least for a few more years.

When the Whitestone girls got up to pay their check, they left behind a piece of paper on the table. I reached over and picked it up.

"What is it?" Marcus asked.

"Looks like an application to Whitestone. Hey, why don't you apply, Marcus?"

"Why don't you eat my shorts?" he calmly replied.

It was mid-August and hot. One good thing about the IHOP: they really cranked up the AC. We had a booth by the window with a view of the street. The cars turning left onto Main Street got blasted by midmorning sun. The drivers all reacted by dropping their sun visors.

"Look: they all do the same thing when they turn," I said. "They all reach up for their sun visors. What are they, programmed like robots? I swear, people are sheep."

Marcus added more sugar to his coffee. "Baa."

That's when it happened. Big Poobs, who to my recollection had never had one truly original idea in his life, spoke up.

"We should do it," he said. "Try to get accepted at Whitestone Prep."

"You, get accepted at Whitestone?" Marcus snorted. "Last time you saw an A or a B, it was in your alphabet soup, genius boy."

Big Poobs shook his head. "Not us. Somebody else. We could, like, invent somebody. A real smart kid. Like, bionic."

I stared at Marcus. "Bionic?"

"Yes!" Poobs was grinning like a jack-o'-lantern. "We can help him apply to Whitestone, see if he gets accepted."

Marcus shook his head. "That's stupid."

At that moment Darla, the waitress, approached the table. "More coffee, boys?"

"No," I told her. "Wait; yes."

Darla peered at me suspiciously but refilled my mug. After she left, I pointed at Big Poobs.

"You are a genius," I told him.

Poobs blinked. "I am?"

I smacked a fist into the palm of my hand.

"Let's do it!" I whispered. "Let's create somebody! Then we'll take that somebody and get him accepted to Whitestone!"

Marcus hesitated. "Create somebody?"

"Yeah, how hard could it be?" I said, studying the application. It was surprisingly short, a single page, front and back. "First thing we need is a name."

"Austin? Brady?" Marcus said.

I shook my head. "Those sound like little-boy names. How about Owen?"

"Or Rowan," Poobs suggested.

"Rowan." We repeated the name, turning it over on our tongues.

"Sounds like a warrior," Marcus mused. "I like it."

"Me too." Carefully, I printed the letters on the application. "Rowan what?"

For some reason that simple question stumped us, almost derailed the project right there and then. Marcus and Poobs threw out some last names—Smith, Johnson, White, Hoffman—but they all sounded lame.

I glanced at the glass window where the letters *IHOP* were stenciled. From where we were sitting, inside the restaurant, the letters appeared in reverse: *POHI.*

"*POHI,*" I stated. "That's IHOP backwards. His name is Rowan Pohi."

Big Poobs thumped the table with his big soft hands. "Rowan Pohi!" He pronounced it like I did: *Pohi.*

"Rowan should have a middle name, shouldn't he?" Marcus said. "How about Ian? Rowan Ian Pohi."

"Bingo." I nodded.

"We're in business, baby!" Poobs exclaimed. In his excitement he knocked over the syrup dispenser, causing some syrup to dribble onto the bottom of the application.

"You idiot!" I snapped. "This has to be handed in!"

"Sorry," Poobs muttered.

I wet a napkin and carefully wiped away the liquid. I did manage to get it off, though it left a faint stain on the paper.

"That will have to do, I guess." I looked at the application. "Sex?"

Marcus laughed. "Obviously!"

I marked the box for Male.

"They want to know where he went to school last year." I drummed the table, thinking hard. "If we say Riverview, we're screwed. If they check for Rowan's name, they'll find nothing and realize that the application is bogus. We better pick some-place far away."

"My mom used to live in a tiny town in Arizona," Marcus put in.

"Yeah?" I looked at him. "Got a name?"

"Piñon," he said. "I went there once. It's really the boonies. Indian country. No green anywhere. Nothing but desert, scor-pions, cactuses."

"Cacti," Poobs corrected him.

I wrote it down. "Rowan went to Piñon High School . . . home of the Stingin' Scorpions."

Poobs rubbed his hands together. "Oh yeah!"

"What's Rowan like?" I said. "We're gonna have to know him real good if we've got any shot at getting him into a school like Whitestone."

"He's a dweeb, like you," Marcus replied.

"I'm serious, numb-nuts."

"Remember Terry Lernihan?" Marcus said.

I nodded. "He moved after fifth grade."

"Lernihan didn't say jack," Marcus remembered. "I hardly ever heard him speak in class. Then one day he comes into school with that refracting telescope he made himself. Took first place in the science fair."

I just looked at him. "And your point is . . ."

"That's what Rowan's like," Marcus continued. "Maybe the dude doesn't say much, but he's smart as hell. A doer, not a talker."

Big Poobs smiled. "Yeah."

"That's a start," I said. "Clubs and activities?"

"Boy Scouts," Marcus suggested. "Definitely put that in. Oh, and National Honor Society."

I nodded. "How about sports?"

"Football!" Big Poobs exclaimed.

"Yesss!"

Football was a very sore subject at Riverview High. It got cut out of the budget last year, along with a bunch of other stuff, so we didn't have a football team anymore. Kids were still pissed off about it. Whitestone Prep had a strong football team; they traveled all around the East Coast to play other private schools. Their school had just added two new turf football fields.

"How about extracurricular activities?" I said.

"Volunteers at soup kitchen."

"Hey, let's not make him into kind some of saint," Poobs warned.

Marcus grinned. "Why not?"

"Sounds good to me," I agreed, and jotted that down.

"Hobbies?"

"Mr. Pohi loves to cook," Poobs suggested with a giggle. "Especially pancakes."

"Are you really that stupid?" I demanded. "That would give it away!"

Poobs sucked his thumb, baby-style. "Sowwy."

"Hey, I skipped this part," I said. "Academics. They want to see Rowan's grades from his old school. We've got to tell them something. Rowan's a good student, right?"

"Damn good!" Big Poobs agreed.

"What's his grade point average?" I asked. "He has to be smart enough to get into a school like Whitestone."

"Four point oh," Poobs declared. "We're talking genius material."

I shook my head. "Let's not get greedy. How about three point six?"

"Yeah, that sounds more realistic," Marcus put in.

My eyes snagged on something I hadn't noticed before, a box on the lower-right-hand corner of the page. Letter of Recommendation.

"Uh-oh," I muttered.

"What?"

"It says he has to send in at least one letter of recommendation." I read out loud: " 'Letter should come from an adult within the school community who has personal knowledge of the applicant—a teacher, coach, or administrator.' "

We stared at each other.

Marcus shrugged. "We'll have to fake one."

"Sign somebody else's name?" Big Poobs looked worried. "Isn't that forgery?"

"We're just goofing," Marcus told him. "Besides, there's no way anybody's gonna trace it back to us."

I gave Marcus a straight look. "Can you do it?"

He smiled. "Sure. Piece o' cake. I'll write a recommendation from his football coach, Ramón García."

Marcus's sudden Spanish accent made Big Poobs snort with laughter.

"You'll have to make up some fake letterhead to write it on," I told Marcus.

He nodded. "Can do. Piñon High School. Home of the Rattlesnakes."

"Home of the Scorpions!" I hissed. "Jeez!"

Marcus smiled lazily. "Scorpions, rattlesnakes . . . what's the diff?"

"There's a huge diff!"

"You can't mail it from here," Big Poobs pointed out. "They put the name of the town on the postmark. So the letter has to be mailed from Piñon, Arizona. If it's from around here, they're going to smell a rat."

"No worries," Marcus said. "My cousin Devon lives out there. I'll write the letter, put it in an envelope, send it to Devon, and have him mail it from there."

"You're good at this," I told Marcus. "A little *too* good."

He bowed. "Thank you very much."

"They want a local mailing address," I said with a shrug. "I'll just use mine."

"So is that it?" Poobs asked eagerly. "Is the application finished?"

"Almost," I told him. On the last line there was a space to sign, which I did now—Rowan I. Pohi—with a flourish and a bold dot above the final *i*. "Done!"

Poobs's face turned serious. "Do you really think we can get him into Whitestone?"

"You better believe it." Marcus theatrically raised his head and began speaking in a mock-solemn tone. "All his life Rowan Pohi has dreamed of going to Whitestone Prep. I ask you: Would you deny this fine young man the chance to make something out of his life? Would you?"

"Nope."

"Nope."

"Nope."

"I count one nope and two dopes," I declared.

I expected Marcus to belt my arm, so when he did I was ready for it. I didn't even flinch.

ON THE WAY HOME I STOPPED AT THE POST OFFICE AND bought a stamp and an envelope. I copied the correct address, tucked the application into the envelope, put on the stamp, and sealed it. When I handed the letter to the clerk, she took a close look at the return address. Then she glanced at me.

I thought she might say *You're Bobby Steele's kid, aren't you?* Instead, she handed the envelope back. "Put it in the mail slot right over there."

I walked to the other side of the room and mailed off Rowan Pohi's application to Whitestone Preparatory School.

We were living on the top floor of a three-story brownstone in a long, narrow apartment. From the small entrance, you passed through the TV room to get to the kitchen. When Mom lived there, the place usually smelled like fried onions or whatever tasty food she had simmering on the stove. Now when you walked in, you smelled only cat litter.

I found my little brother, Cody, in the den, crumpled in front of the TV with Turf, our cat, dozing beside him. Mrs. Richards watched Cody in the afternoon; she must have let him in. Cody had a feather in the back of his hair, sticking up Indian-style.

Not too long after Mom left, Cody started insisting that he was 100 percent Native American. I knew for a fact he didn't have any Indian blood in him, not one single drop, but I didn't argue. I figured if it made him feel better, what the heck, no harm, no foul. Every morning, Cody put a feather in his hair when he got dressed. Once in a while, if my father wasn't around, I even dabbed some war paint (green face cream Mom left behind) on his face.

"Bobby, how many days till I go to school?" He asked the question without taking his eye off the cartoon he was watching—*SpongeBob.*

"A week till kindergarten," I told him. "You getting excited?"

"Yeah." Though he didn't sound excited.

I went into the kitchen. My father had a regular schedule for supper, and we followed it religiously. Wednesday was spaghetti night, so it was my night to cook. I used premade sauce, the kind you buy in a jar, but I doctored it up with fried onions and garlic to improve the taste, the way Mom showed me once. After that I filled a pot halfway full with water for pasta and turned on the oven to warm up the garlic bread. Then I made the salad. My father liked to eat at six o'clock sharp, which suited me fine.

He came home looking hot and grimy, like he usually did after work. My father owned CarWorks, an auto-repair shop on the corner of Fifteenth and Remington. There were three other mechanics and three lifts at his garage. I had a part-time job there, mostly doing oil changes and vacuuming out cars, and earned enough money to buy things I needed.

"Hi," I said. "We can eat whenever."

"Okay, gimme ten minutes." He hung his keys on the hook next to the refrigerator and headed into the bathroom. A moment later I heard the shower turn on.

During supper we watched our cat chase a housefly around the room. We got Turf at the hardware store a little more than a year ago. Cody, Mom, and I were walking through the gardening section and found a small gray cat sound asleep on a green square. The sign above said ARTIFICIAL TURF SALE. One of the clerks noticed our interest and mentioned that the cat needed a home, so Mom agreed to make her part of our family. Cody named her Turf.

My father reached for a piece of garlic bread and pulled it apart. Cody pushed his spaghetti around on the plate. We had run out of Kraft Parmesan cheese. "I can't eat it without cheese," Cody complained.

"It don't matter," my father said. "Eat."

Doesn't matter, I mentally corrected him. My father's bad grammar really bugged me.

I favored my father: pale blue eyes, sandy hair, freckles, and long legs. With his compact limbs, dark eyes, and curly black hair, Cody looked like Mom. A *lot* like Mom. The spitting image, isn't that what they say? It was freaky. No matter how many times I looked at Cody, I always got a little jolt. It was like having a mini-Mom in the house. It must have been weird for my father too.

"Today I was working on a 'ninety-nine Camry," he was saying. "Do whatever you gotta do, the owner told me when he dropped off the car. That's what he said: Do whatever you gotta do. Car needed a new water pump, so I got one from my supplier and tell Jimmy to put it in. Cost a hundred and fifty, with labor, but when the guy comes to pick up the car, he goes apeshit, says I'm charging way too much. Says, 'I didn't authorize it, and I'm not paying.'"

Cody grinned. "Apeshit!"

My brother was like a myna bird when it came to repeating my father's curses. If he heard a swear even once, it got stuck in his head forever.

"Don't say that," I told him.

"But Daddy did."

I ignored him and glanced at my father. "So what did you do?"

"I says, Okay, fine," my father said. "You wanna play stupid, I can play stupid too. I had Jimmy take out the new water pump and put back the old one. What a fruitcake!"

While my father was talking I tried not to stare at his hands, which were bigger and darker than the rest of his body. It was as if a larger man's hands had somehow been grafted onto his arms. At CarWorks, my father's hands got coated in every kind of oil, lubricant, and engine grime you could imagine. After twenty years, all those greasy fluids had soaked into his skin. He used a special soap that washed off the filth, but only the top layer. The other stuff was still there just below the surface. His hands would never be deep-down clean.

Turf finally caught the fly she had been chasing. She curled up a few feet from the table, allowing us to hear the sound of the trapped fly buzzing around in her mouth. You'd think Turf would swallow it, but she kept that fly in there, alive, flying around. Cody giggled.

"That is one wacked-out cat," my father declared.

After supper we cleaned the kitchen. He turned on the Sox game. I put on my gym shoes and went out for a run.

Running right after supper seems like a bad idea, but it

didn't bother me. You've got an iron stomach, Mom used to say. My belly might be stuffed with spaghetti and garlic bread, but I didn't want to miss running, not for anything. It was the one time of day that really felt like mine.

We didn't live in the worst part of the city, but our neighborhood had definitely seen better days. Running down Robertson I passed two liquor stores, a pawnshop, and a bank, followed by Luquer's, a secondhand clothes store. The next block was a row of apartment buildings and then a huge, faded brick building.

Welcome to my high school.

The school was named Riverview High, except a few years ago they erected two wide office buildings on the west side, eliminating any view of the river. I guess nobody thought to change the name. Through the chainlink fence you could see the parking lot all torn up by construction. The school board passed an improvement plan to add parking spaces and a running track, but it got halted last year due to the newest round of budget cuts. In two weeks I would begin my sophomore year.

I passed the school, crossed onto Cherry, and headed south toward People's Park, which ran along the reservoir. I did four long blocks, then crossed diagonally through Wilson Square before heading west on Birch. It was a clear evening, and I found myself chasing a lazy red sun.

Some people do complicated things when they run: monitor

their stride, breathe in rhythm, and keep their hands low. For me, running has always felt as natural as walking or breathing: I just ran. I never thought a lick about it. And I was fast too, faster than any kid in my grade.

The reservoir appeared on the left. Sunlight glistened on the water while I ran along the boardwalk. This was my favorite part of the day. I pretended the lake was mine. Out of the corner of my eye I glimpsed ripples in the water, probably a fish rising to the surface to feed. Maybe later I'd take my imaginary girlfriend out in my imaginary boat and do some fishing. Fish like to feed at twilight. I got a whiff of chicken cooking on a grill, and the smell made my mouth water, even though I'd already eaten.

I ran along the reservoir: stride, stride, stride, stride. A line of huge ancient elms blocked any view of the sunset, but glancing in the other direction I could see the distant buildings of Whitestone up on the hill, looking down over the city.

I tried not to think about Whitestone, but I couldn't help it. Beyond the hype and the snob factor, it really was a terrific school with A-list teachers. *First class all the way,* Mom used to say, and I had no reason to doubt her. More than once I wondered if I might fit in better at a school like that. At Riverview, kids called you geekster or nerdling if you dared show any interest in history or literature, so I had to hide that side of myself. Kids at Whitestone really wanted to learn, from what I'd heard, so there was nothing wrong with paying attention or speaking up in class.

Two girls waved as I passed a girls' softball game, and I waved back. I felt airy and loose and free. I wasn't winded either, not even a little bit. I felt like I could keep on going forever. It was a perfect August evening. At that moment, running in the opposite direction from home, feeling it get farther and farther away, I could almost understand why Mom had kept going and didn't turn back.

I passed Jitterbug's Coffee Shoppe and spotted the sign for Vanderbilt Boulevard half a block ahead. That was my signal to turn right.

I wasn't really angry at Mom for leaving. I couldn't hold it against her. Not after what my father did. I could understand why she skipped out on us. Almost. But I couldn't do what she did. I didn't feel like I was better than her; just different. Whenever I went out to run, I curved like a boomerang, traveling far and wide but then bending around and heading toward home. I always came back.

THREE

THREE DAYS LATER I FOUND IN OUR MAILBOX A SLENDER envelope with a single sheet of paper inside.

Dear Rowan,

We appreciate your interest in Whitestone. During the past two years we have worked hard to bring in a more diverse student population. After carefully reviewing your application, plus the enthusiastic letter of recommendation from Mr. Ramón García, the admissions committee has decided that you would be a strong addition to our learning community. Congratulations, Rowan! Allow me to extend my personal welcome to Whitestone Preparatory School.

A detailed letter will follow. Please do not lose it!

This letter will contain important information pertaining to necessary medical forms, the academic calendar, scheduled tuition payments, and school uniforms. The first day of school is August 26. I look forward to meeting you then.

Sincerely,

Melody Ryder
Director of Admissions

PS: This acceptance is conditional upon our receiving a satisfactory transcript (including grades) from your previous school in a timely fashion.

Sitting on the cement stairs, I slowly reread the letter. A car alarm started beeping, but I didn't even look up. When I was convinced that the letter was real, I ran inside, grabbed my phone, and texted Marcus and Big Poobs.

Urgent. Meet at IHOP 3:30.

When I got there it was after the lunch hour but too early for dinner, so the restaurant was nearly empty. The hostess let us have our favorite booth by the window.

"He got in!" I blurted out.

The blank way Marcus and Big Poobs stared at me, you would have thought I was speaking Mandarin Chinese.

"He got accepted!" I repeated.

"Who?"

"Rowan! He got accepted at Whitestone!"

Marcus smiled. "Bullshit."

Big Poobs wasn't buying it either, so I had to whip out the acceptance letter. They lunged at it like two piranhas hitting a piece of bloody meat—I swear, they practically ripped it in half—and still didn't believe me until they held that letter in their hands and read it with their own eyes.

Then all three of us erupted. We started laughing, high-fiving, power-bumping, whooping it up so much the waitress gave us an evil look and marched toward our table.

"Shut up!" I hissed at Marcus and Big Poobs. Today of all days I didn't want to get thrown out.

"Sorry," I mumbled to our waitress.

She glared at me but took our drink order and left.

"That is money!" Marcus softly exclaimed, pointing at the letter.

"Not bad." I was trying to be cool but couldn't keep the goofy grin off my face.

Big Poobs looked both happy and bewildered. "What the . . . ? I mean, how did—?"

"It worked!" Marcus whispered softly. "We did it! Rowan rules!"

At that moment four Whitestone students entered the restaurant and settled in a few tables away. The sight of four actual flesh-and-blood Stonys caused us to lose it completely. We collapsed into uncontrollable laughter, especially Big Poobs. He howled silently until he had tears running down his fat face.

"But now what?" Marcus finally said.

The waitress brought our drinks, and for the next minute we sipped without saying a word. We didn't know what to do next, not really. Deep down none of us ever thought Rowan would actually get accepted to Whitestone.

"I propose a toast," Big Poobs said, lifting his root beer. "To Rowan Pohi!"

"Hear, hear!"

I fired a finger gun at Marcus. "That letter of recommendation from Ramón García did the trick."

"Yeah, *Señor* García laid it on pretty thick," Marcus admitted. "Did you know that Rowan started a tutoring program for underprivileged kids?"

I grinned. "Nice touch!"

Marcus studied the letter. "Did you read this to the end, Bobby? It sounds like Rowan's not really accepted until they see his grades and transcripts from his last school."

I sighed. "Yeah, well, that ain't gonna happen."

"His last school was right here," Big Poobs declared, rubbing his belly. "You know, I could go for a stack of pancakes right now."

"Is food your number one priority in life?" I demanded.

"Pretty much, yeah," Poobs admitted.

Marcus slurped the dregs of his drink. "So what should we do with him?"

Poobs blinked. "Who?"

"Rowan Pohi, genius."

It hit me: at that moment we were talking about Rowan like he was a real live person.

"I was thinking we're going to have to, like, deactivate him," Marcus suggested. "Not right away but, you know, pretty soon."

"Why?" Poobs asked.

I made a face. "Jeez, Marcus, let the poor kid live a little. He was just born a couple days ago!"

The waitress refilled our drinks and we kept talking like that for the next half-hour, all of us jacked up on sugar and adrenaline and the realization that against all odds our impossible plan had worked.

Here's what I didn't say to my friends: In a strange kind of way, I wasn't surprised to read that letter. Not really. Because the moment I wrote the name Rowan Pohi on that application, I heard a little electronic *blip.* Not just inside my brain, but out loud. Like the sound you hear when an instant message suddenly appears on your computer screen.

Like: *I'm here.*

FOUR

AT QUARTER TO FIVE I LEFT THE RESTAURANT AND HEADED home. The heat had finally broken; the summer air was soft and sweet. I was just passing Luquer's, the used-clothing store, when I noticed the girl coming toward me on the sidewalk. She was tall and leggy, with a purple headband and an impressive mane of hair, blond. I recognized her as that Whitestone girl who'd seen sitting in a booth with her friends at the IHOP a few days earlier.

Even from a distance you could see how pretty she was. Maybe she recognized me from the IHOP, because she flashed me a sly smile. Nice. I was still riding high from the Rowan Pohi thing and figured the least I could do was introduce myself. But then I tried to imagine it, playing the scene out in my head.

Hi.

Hey.

26

Didn't I see you at the IHOP the other day?

Uh-huh. I'm Melissa. What's your name?

Bobby. Bobby Steele.

Talk about a conversation stopper! My father and I had the same name. It wouldn't be surprising if she had read about my father in the newspaper or heard someone mention his name. I didn't want to take that risk, so I dropped my eyes and swung past her, like a guy who had more important things on his mind.

My father grilled sirloin tips for supper. The deck wasn't big enough for a table, so we ate in the kitchen. I turned on the fan and lifted the windows to let in the summer air. While we ate we could hear Spanish music drifting up from one of the apartments below ours.

"The Indians hunted meat," Cody was saying.

"Don't talk with your mouth full," my father told him.

Cody swallowed and gulped down some milk. "They used a bow and arrow to kill some cows."

The feather in Cody's hair was tilting; I reached over and straightened it.

"Not cows," I told him. "They hunted buffalo and antelope."

"Can I go to the bead store?" Cody asked. "Please, Dad?"

My father grunted. "You got money?"

Cody nodded eagerly. "I still got ten dollars from my birthday!"

My father glanced over at me. "Maybe Bobby will take you."

I groaned. "I'm busy."

Cody gave me a sulky look. "That's what you always say."

"Well, I am."

After supper, my father went to an AA meeting. Ever since *it* happened, he had been court-ordered to stay away from booze and go to at least three AA meetings per week. He had a special form he had to get signed to show he was there.

Later that night Cody appeared at my bedroom door, looking a little forlorn.

"You didn't read me a story, Bobby."

I sighed. "Oh, all right. C'mon."

I closed my book and followed him into his room. "Those PJs are way too hot. They're for winter."

"No they're not," Cody insisted.

"They'll make you all sweaty." I rummaged through his drawer until I found a pair of summer-weight PJs. "Put these on."

"Okay. Don't look, Bobby."

I turned around to give him some privacy and glanced at his bed. He had already picked out the book he wanted to read: *Horton Hatches the Egg.* It was the same worn copy Mom read to me when I was little.

I sat on his bed, leaning back against the headboard. Cody leaned against me as I started reading the Dr. Seuss book. He laughed at the pictures, and chimed in whenever we came to the part where Horton says, "An elephant's faithful one hundred percent!"

Then we came to the part that talks about Mayzie, the lazy mother of the bird egg, who is on some kind of extended vacation. She's having so much fun chilling out at the beach that she decides she's never going to return to the egg to take care of it.

Cody got very still.

"You okay?" I asked him.

He nodded. But after that he didn't laugh at the pictures. And next time we came to the part where he could chime in, he said nothing.

"You want me to keep going?"

Quietly: "I don't care."

"We can stop, if you want."

"It's almost done," he said.

I finished reading the book. Cody climbed off me and slid under the covers. He grabbed his stuffed squirrel and turned toward the wall.

I put my hand on his back. "You miss Mom?"

Eyes closed, he tucked the squirrel under his chin. I waited for him to say something, but he didn't. It broke my heart that he didn't answer me one way or another. I couldn't give him Mom, but I wanted to give him something. Anything.

I cleared my throat. "Okay, I'll take you to the bead store."

He turned to look at me. "You will?"

I nodded.

"When?" he asked. "Tomorrow?"

"One day this week. Thursday."

He grinned. "I got ten dollars."

"I know."

I told him good night and went to my bedroom.

When I closed my eyes that night, Mom's picture rose into my mind. She had been gone more than a year now, but I remembered her like she'd just left this morning. The smell of her perfume. The way she hummed while she was cooking. Seems like she was always frying a big skillet of onions in the kitchen. There was a big dark mole on her back—Mom's raisin, that's what me and Cody called it. I remembered the dreamy, faraway look in her eyes when she stirred her morning coffee.

And I will never forget what my father did to her.

FIVE

My PARENTS ARGUED A LOT, BUT LATE LAST SPRING THEIR fights turned nasty. They fought about money, mostly. Mom had gotten laid off at the school where she worked as a special education teacher. Dad had work troubles too. An inspector said the ventilation system at his repair shop didn't meet city code and shut down the shop for two months. Dad got really pissed. A royal rip-off, he insisted, but finally he realized it was cheaper to update the system than fight City Hall, so that's what he did. It cost him close to ten thousand dollars.

On that particular night, I was in my bedroom, trying to tune out their fighting while I worked on an essay I had to write for English about *The Lord of the Flies.* Jack and Ralph. Dark and light. The conch shell and Piggy's glasses.

What really happened in our apartment that night? It took two days before I had a general idea. Certain things I witnessed myself. Certain things were told to me. But certain things I didn't find out about until I read them in the newspaper. The events that night never formed themselves into a connected story with a beginning, a middle, and an end. Instead I was left with a list of facts.

For supper that night Mom had splurged on Alaskan king crab legs.

The crab cost $14.99 per pound.

She was ironing a blouse when my father came home.

He got in her face for spending so much money on food.

Usually Mom backed down when they had a fight.

That night she didn't back down.

They started screaming at each other.

Bellowing so loud the neighbors heard it.

My father grabbed the hot iron.

Pressed it to Mom's bare upper arm.

A piercing scream from the kitchen.

I ran from my room. Took in the scene.

The ironing board upended on the floor.

A bad new smell in the kitchen. Like seared meat.

Mom bent over the sink.

Sobbing.

He had her arm under the kitchen faucet, running water over the injured skin.

He was talking to her. Talking gently.

She couldn't stop crying.

They argued again, almost tenderly this time.

Him: You need to go to the hospital.

Her: I'm okay.

Him: I'm taking you to the hospital.

Her: No, I'll be okay by tomorrow.

Him: You're not okay. I'm taking you to the emergency room.

Her: I'll be okay, Bobby.

Finally she gave in.

She told me: "You're the man of the house. Keep an eye on Cody."

By some miracle, my brother slept through the whole thing.

They left in a taxi.

I didn't know what else to do, so I turned on the TV.

They came home two hours later.

Mom's arm covered in gauze from the elbow up.

A trying-to-be-brave smile on her face.

"It looked worse than it is. The doctor said I'll be fine."

Dad poured himself a drink. Old Smuggler Scotch.

Turned on the TV to catch the end of the baseball game, but it was over.

Fifteen minutes later the doorbell rang.

Two police, one tall, one short.

"I need to speak to Robert Steele."

My father came to the door.

"Mr. Steele?"

"That's me."

"We have a warrant for your arrest."

"But I don't want to press charges!" Mom protested.

"It's out of your hands, ma'am. This is a criminal matter. Sorry."

They handcuffed my father and took him away.

For a few weeks our life at home was like a circus.

A stream of strangers tramping through our apartment.

Police who needed to talk to Mom.

A lawyer who needed to talk to Dad.

Two social workers who needed to talk to me and Cody.

I didn't want to talk to anyone. Not even Marcus or Big Poobs.

One day I had had enough. If I didn't get out, I would start throwing things at people.

So I went for a walk. Bought the local paper at the newsstand.

There he was. On the front page.

My father.

Dark circles under his eyes.

Looking like the kind of man who really could do such a thing.

The headline: IRON STEELE.

I sped through the article, soaking up the missing facts and details nobody had bothered to tell me.

Marilyn Steele suffered second-degree burns.

Robert Steele was charged with aggravated assault, a felony.

The article quoted a nurse in the emergency room: "The pattern of the iron had been branded into the victim's skin."

A man approached the newsstand. He plunked down two quarters and grinned at Ivan, the guy who sells the papers.

"Now, that is a man who knows how to make a good impression!"

The two of them shared a laugh.

Dad didn't want a trial, so he copped a plea.

Except I didn't call him Dad. After what he did that night, I would never think of him as Dad again.

He was sentenced to ninety days in the county jail.

Mom brought us to see him every Sunday afternoon. Trust me: it feels surreal to visit your father in jail, but it's amazing how fast you get used to the routine. We had to go through a metal detector. One time Cody pulled a plastic pistol from his pocket, just a toy squirt gun, but the guard confiscated it and didn't give it back when we left.

My father looked tired. He grew a little beard, sort of a goatee thing, but I didn't much like it, and I don't think Cody did either.

I don't know whether Mom liked it or not. I didn't know what she was thinking. While my father tried to talk to us she sat without speaking, a tight little half smile on her face.

The doctor removed the bandage on her upper arm. She said she was completely healed, but the skin looked different—darker and shinier—than the surrounding area.

With time credited for good behavior, my father got released in sixty-five days. We had to talk to the social worker a few more times after he came home, but it seemed like things might finally go back to normal. Mom got rehired at school. My father went back to brake jobs and timing belts at his repair shop. He also had to take an anger management class.

One afternoon I came home. The apartment felt different. On the kitchen counter there was a note with a gold wedding band sitting on top of it. Like a tiny paperweight to prevent that note from blowing away.

Dear Bobby and Cody,
I love you so much
goodbye
Mom

When my father came home from work, he read the note.

"Well, boys, your mother's left and gone."

"Where?" Cody asked in a small voice.

"I don't know."

"Is she coming back?" he squeaked.

"I doubt it." He shook his head. "Looks like we're on our own."

He never talked about her after that.

SIX

IT WAS HARDEST FOR CODY. HE CRIED ALMOST EVERY NIGHT.
It wasn't easy listening to that.

My brother began acting peculiar too. For instance, if he and I were walking in the city, and Cody saw some woman who looked even remotely like Mom, he'd start hyperventilating with excitement, jumping up and down.

"I see Mom! Look, Bobby! She's right over there!"

"No, she's not," I'd tell him. He wouldn't believe me, so I'd have to bring him closer until he could see for himself that it wasn't Mom.

He pulled this stunt again and again until finally I couldn't take it anymore. One afternoon when he swore he saw Mom, I grabbed his shoulder and dragged him to where the woman was standing.

"See? What did I tell you? That's not Mom!"

The woman looked at me, startled.

"But it looked like Mom," he whimpered.

"Stop saying that!" I yelled. "Mom's gone! Get that through your head."

Cody burst into tears. He cried all the way home.

Next morning was the first time he showed up at breakfast with a feather in his hair, sticking up in back.

My father sat up straight. "Well, I'll be."

"I'm a Indian boy," Cody declared.

My father rubbed his chin.

"Is that so?"

"Uh-huh." Cody nodded. "My mommy lives in a tepee."

Wacky stuff. But after he started wearing that feather, Cody stopped "finding" Mom on the street. Which was a big relief.

SEVEN

THE POLICE CONFISCATED THE IRON. EVIDENCE, THEY SAID.
Eventually they returned it, but I never saw Mom use it again.
Or my father either. He could rebuild a transmission but wouldn't
be caught dead ironing a shirt, so that iron stayed in the closet.

I didn't know what to think about what my father did. Many
times I tried hard to think about it, but I never got very far. I'm not
naive. I realize that very few married couples live in happily-ever-
after-ville. Lots of husbands find ways to ruin their marriages.

Drinking themselves silly.

Cheating with other women.

Gambling away the food money.

Abandoning their families.

Beating their wives.

But a man who burns his wife with a hot iron? Who leaves
an impression of that iron on her skin?

One morning I woke to discover that during the night my life had divided itself into two pieces: Life Before and Life After. Life After did have its pluses. With Mom gone, we ate more meat and fewer vegetables. The guy at Movie Palace let me rent R-rated movies—my father didn't care. Sunday morning my father didn't drag us to church either, like Mom used to do.

Life After felt different in other ways too. After my father got out of jail and Mom left, I didn't feel quite so relaxed when he was in the house. Jacqueline, a social worker, came every so often to check on Cody and me for the first few months. She was a friendly lady who smelled really nice and always brought a bag of butterscotch candies. Jacqueline must have sensed something because one day she asked me: "Are you afraid of your father, Bobby?"

"No," I told her.

That was true, though it wasn't the whole story. I was definitely more aware, more watchful, around my father. Even when he was asleep down the hallway in his bedroom, even when I was asleep, some part of me stayed alert.

I'm not saying that I considered him some kind of monster. I knew my father loved me and my brother. But facts are facts: he hurt Mom. Now that my eyes had been opened, I couldn't completely shut them.

Mom once told me he'd never physically hurt her before

that, ever. So what was the deal? How had he gone from Dad Before to Father After? Was this one of those once-in-a-lifetime things, a freak event that would never be repeated? Or did it signal some kind of ominous crack in his foundation?

One thing's for sure: my father proved that your life can change for the worse because of one thing you do, one act you commit. Sometimes I wondered if it could also work the other way around. Could you do one reckless thing, throw one desperate Hail Mary pass to transform your life from Before to After in a good way?

My father was trying hard to clean up his act. He had finished his anger management classes and stopped drinking. Still, I did have nagging worries. I didn't obsess about it, but, well, maybe one day he would lose his temper again and try to hurt me. Or worse, my brother. That was not going to happen. Not Cody. Not on my watch.

EIGHT

EIGHT

On Thursdays I worked five hours at my father's garage. I didn't help on any of the serious repairs. Mostly he kept me busy doing oil changes and vacuuming out the cars before we gave them back to the customers. I knew how to rotate tires too, though he didn't have me do that yet. All in all it wasn't bad work. The other mechanics treated me fine. I got paid twelve dollars an hour, off the books, which was more than I could earn anywhere else. And I needed the money.

That afternoon I took Cody to the bead store, like I'd promised. Its real name was Kopsky's Gifts and Novelties, but Cody called it the bead store because there was a huge section devoted to beads for making jewelry. It was by far Cody's favorite store. It wasn't so much the beads that interested Cody as the large selection of Indian stuff.

As I stepped into the store, a wave of incense smell washed over me, sickeningly sweet. Mr. Kopsky stood behind the counter, arms folded. He was a big, lumpy man with thick black hair, and he wasn't exactly a barrel of laughs. I had been to his store at least a dozen times and had never once seen him smile.

Cody made a beeline for the far wall, where a sign proclaimed GENUINE NATIVE AMERICAN CRAFTS. I wasn't convinced about the *genuine* part. A few items looked real; for instance, some arrowheads displayed in a locked glass cabinet, but there were lots of cheap items (wallets, leather moccasins, purses woven from beads, toy headdresses) that could have been made by anyone.

Naturally, my brother ignored the inexpensive stuff and zeroed in on a necklace made of porcupine quills and three large bear claws. The kid had good taste—the necklace looked like the real deal. There was a tiny white price tag lying face-down on the display table; when I flipped it over, I almost gagged.

"A hundred bucks!"

Cody gave me a pleading look. "I want it."

"You can't afford it." I steered him to the bins with the low-priced items. "You better stay over here."

Cody twisted his neck to look over his shoulder. "But I want that necklace!"

"Then you have to save your money. You can do that, but that means you won't be able to buy anything today."

I knew Cody pretty well. I figured there was no way he'd be able to leave that store without buying some kind of treat.

"Oh, okay." He sighed.

I left him looking at smudge sticks, miniature drums, and dream catchers while I wandered around the store. A few minutes later I went back to check on my brother.

"Made up your mind?" I asked him.

He showed me a small toy hatchet decorated with feathers.

"It costs ten dollars," he said.

It was a flimsy thing that would likely break in less than a week. I felt a pang in my gut. "Is that what you want?"

He nodded without a lot of enthusiasm.

"We can keep looking," I told him.

He spun the hatchet in his hands. "No, it's pretty cool."

We took the little hatchet to the front of the store. Cody handed his ten-dollar bill to Mr. Kopsky, and we left.

When we got back home, I checked our mail slot. I was excited to find a thick envelope from Whitestone Preparatory School addressed to Rowan Pohi. I took it up to our apartment, went to my bedroom, and closed the door so I could read in privacy.

The envelope contained a personal welcome from Dr. Paul LeClerc, the headmaster of the upper school. I thought that title sounded very exclusive and private-schoolish; for some reason, it made me picture Hogwarts. There was also a form asking for certain information (phone number, Social Security number) that I had left off the original application. I found a tuition bill to the tune of $13,848. I let out a soft whistle. As if to soften that blow, the envelope also contained lots of Whitestone paraphernalia: car stickers, a pen, a mini-pennant, even a little stack of Whitestone sticky notes.

At the IHOP my buddies were delighted when I showed them all the Whitestone loot. Big Poobs waved the little pennant back and forth. "Rah-rah White-stone! This is awe-some!"

"Did you check out that tuition bill?" I said. "They want about fourteen thousand bucks."

Big Poobs smiled. "Piece of cake. Rowan's got a rich uncle, I heard."

I made a sour face. "Rowan's got squat, and you know it. They want his Social Security number and his phone number too. I can just imagine them calling my house and having my father pick up the phone. You want to give them your phone number? Huh?"

Marcus blinked at me. "Are you saying—"

I shrugged. "What I'm saying is . . . Look, I haven't had so much fun since my cousin Corey let me shave off half his hair, but—I don't know—maybe this is where we get off."

Poobs stuck out his lower lip. He picked up the Whitestone

car sticker and held it against the window. "But this stuff is hilarious. This is a letter from the *headmaster.*"

"If you worked at Whitestone," Marcus told Poobs, "you'd be the bellymaster."

Poobs grinned and patted his stomach. "Damn straight!"

For a moment nobody said anything. Then Marcus nodded. "Bobby's right. Time to pull the plug. Soon. Let's do it tomorrow. Let's give Rowan one more day on this earth."

So we agreed to wait until tomorrow, only it didn't turn out that way.

I had barely gotten home from the IHOP when Marcus sent me a text:

Rowan's sick. Stomachache or . . . ?

Big Poobs: Might B Ebola virus   that's the one that turns your brain to diarea

Big Poobs was a terrible speller, but I got the point. I sat on our stoop and fired off a reply.

Relax. Rowans fine. Chill.

Big Poobs: Not sure about that   Rowan said take him to the hospital so we did

Marcus: Yeah we're at the ER right now

Now that I could see where this was heading, I decided to relax and go along for the ride. What else could I do?

Me: How is he?

Marcus: *BAD*   They took him to ICU

Big Poobs: Temp is up   face is hot

Marcus: His nurse is hot!!! A real QT

Me: Will he get better?

Big Poobs: Worse

Marcus: Doc says his pulse is slowing . . . he's bleeding from his ears

Me: TMI!

Marcus: LMAO

Marcus: Shhhhhh   critical condition

Big Poobs: Emergency! Cardiac arrest!

Nobody texted anything for a full minute. I tried to be patient, but the suspense was killing me.

Me: What the %&! is happening????

Marcus: Cant see the letters on the keyboard

Me: Why not?

Marcus: 2 many tears

I was chuckling now, despite myself.

Me: Is he dead?

Poobs: Yeah   Gdby Rowan

Marcus: Dude fought hard right to the end

Poobs: gr8fl I knew him

I paused, not sure what to say.

Me: What now?

Another long pause. Finally . . .

Big Poobs: We gotta bury him before he gets riga mortis

I was thinking, *Bury Rowan? How?*

Me: Where?

Marcus: Meet at 10 2nite crnr of sibberson and spence

Me: OK

Marcus: Sad day

Me: ur messed ^

Marcus: ☺

Me: Xtremely messed ^

Marcus: Rowan's last words: MY #1 REGRET IS ILL NEVER GET

2 B A STONY

NINE

THE ABANDONED LOT WAS CORDONED OFF WITH HIGH chainlink fencing. For years we'd heard rumors that they were going to turn this lot into a park for kids, a farmers' market, a community garden—but nothing happened. Nothing ever did. The lighting was bad. At night it felt dangerous, the perfect place to get mugged, though I'd actually never heard of anything bad going on here. It was just a forgotten square of the city.

We followed the fencing until we came to a part that had been lifted. The three of us shimmied underneath.

"Think this is okay?" Big Poobs murmured.

I glanced up and down the street; the only thing you could see was a line of parked cars. "What's wrong with it?"

"I dunno," Poobs said. "It just seems so . . . exposed. Couldn't we at least find someplace over there in the corner?"

Marcus snorted. "You gonna come every Sunday to put flowers on his grave? It's good enough, genius."

"I guess."

We crouched down. Marcus had brought some sticks that we used to start digging a small grave. Big Poobs turned on a tiny flashlight and set it up so we could see what we were doing.

"This dirt is like cement," I muttered. "How deep should we go?"

"Four inches," said Big Poobs.

I laughed. "Why exactly four inches? Why not three? Or five?"

"Four," he repeated.

"Poor guy," Marcus said. "Dude didn't last very long once he took sick."

"You guys are even more twisted than I thought," I told him.

Big Poobs scooped out one last handful of dirt. "Done."

"Where's Rowan's stuff?" Marcus asked me.

"Here." I handed him two envelopes: the acceptance letter and the information packet.

"I'm keeping the Whitestone pen," Poobs announced.

"No, you're not," Marcus told him. "We agreed: everything goes into the grave."

"Oh, all right."

Poobs dropped in the pen, and we covered Rowan's things with the dirt we had dug out. The two envelopes and all that loosened dirt pushed the grave an inch higher than the surrounding ground. Marcus stood and used his boot to tamp it down.

Big Poobs shined his flashlight up at himself, casting weird shadows on his face.

"This isn't how I pictured it. I mean, how we'd bury him."

"What's wrong now?" Marcus asked impatiently.

Poobs glanced around again. "I don't know. It's such a crappy place."

Marcus swore. "What did you expect, Arlington National Cemetery?"

"Just someplace better than this," Poobs murmured. "I mean, for me, it wouldn't matter. I honestly don't care where they bury me. But Rowan was different from us. Rowan had a chance to be somebody."

"Rowan was a figment of our imagination," Marcus shot back. "C'mon, let's finish this."

"Okay," I said. "Does anybody want to say anything?"

There was a long pause. For some fool reason a wave of sadness—the real kind—washed over me.

"He will be missed," Big Poobs finally said.

"Uh-huh," I agreed. My throat felt so tight I didn't trust myself to say more than that.

"Bye, Rowan," Big Poobs said softly.

We started to turn away, but Poobs grabbed my arm.

"No one will even know it's here," he said. "Shouldn't we mark it somehow?"

"How?"

Big Poobs crouched down. Using one of the sharp sticks, he wrote three letters in the dirt. Then he stood and flashed a narrow beam of light onto the ground.

R I P

I stood there without moving.

Rowan Ian Pohi.

Rest In Peace.

TEN

SUPPER ON SATURDAY NIGHT WAS HOT DOGS PLUS MACA-
roni and cheese. My father didn't have to work on the weekends,
so we ate earlier than usual. Saturdays he usually went to a
seven o'clock AA meeting.

The weather forecast called for T-storms that would bring
in cooler temperatures, but the storms hadn't come. It was one
of the warmest days of the summer.

"Did you buy Popsicles?" I asked my father as he was
cooking.

He shook his head. "What I would really love right now is a
cold beer."

That jolted me. "But you—"

"I know I can't have one." He rolled the hot dogs in the fry
pan. "But that don't mean I don't want one somethin' fierce."

Doesn't mean, I mentally corrected him, though I didn't say it out loud.

He ripped a paper towel off the roll and used it to wipe his face. "Haven't you ever wanted something real bad even though you know you can't have it?"

"Yeah," I admitted. A picture of that tall Whitestone girl flashed through my head.

"Well, all right, then." He turned off the heat under the pasta. "Tell Cody it's time to set the table."

I found Cody in his bedroom. Today the feather stuck in his hair was from a pigeon, a germ-riddled bird if ever there was one. He stood with his back to me, bending over the middle drawer of his bureau. When he heard me come in, he quickly closed the drawer.

"What are you doing?" I asked.

"Nothing."

That got me suspicious, but I didn't let on. "Wash your hands. You need to set the table."

Ten minutes later it was time to eat. While my father and Cody were sitting down, I slipped out of the kitchen and into Cody's bedroom. I opened the middle drawer of his bureau.

Son of a bitch, there it was.

The bear-claw Indian necklace.

The little thief.

I stormed back to the table and got in Cody's face. "Do you have something to tell me?" I demanded.

I gave him a moment to come clean, but he said nothing. From his innocent expression you would have thought he was rocking a halo instead of a pigeon feather on his head.

"What's wrong?" my father asked.

When I took the necklace out of my pocket, Cody was outraged.

"That's mine! You took it from my room!"

"You stole it!" I yelled.

"I did not!" Cody shouted back.

"He stole it from Kopsky's bead store," I explained to my father.

"Give it here," he ordered.

He fingered the necklace with his big, dark hands. Then he glanced up at me. "Didn't Grandma give him ten dollars?"

I folded my arms. "Yeah, but that necklace cost a hundred. He spent the ten on a toy tomahawk."

"Uh-uh!" Desperately, Cody shook his head.

My father gave him a level look. "Did you steal this?"

Cody's lower lip trembled. "But—"

My father cut him off in midsentence. "But nothing! You

know what they do to people who steal? Huh? They put them in jail! You want to go to jail?"

Like me? he could have added, but I guess he didn't have to.

Cody wasn't completely stupid. "They don't put little kids in jail."

"They can put you in juvenile detention." My father glared at Cody. "That's no walk in the park, mister."

What would Mom do? I wondered. Immediately I knew the answer.

"We gotta go to the store so you can give it back," I told Cody. "You've got to tell Mr. Kopsky you took the necklace, and apologize."

Cody's eyes were wide with panic. "I can't go back there! He'll be so mad! He'll yell at me!"

My father swallowed a bite of macaroni. "You should've thought about that when you stole the necklace. Bobby's right. You're going back right after supper."

"No!" Cody protested.

"Be quiet," my father said sharply. "I've heard enough from you."

Cody had lost his appetite, but my father made him sit there while we finished eating. By the time we had cleaned up the kitchen it was five o'clock; on Saturdays the bead store stayed open until six. I put the necklace into a small paper bag. I found my brother in a corner of the den, trying to look invisible. Turf was curled up nearby. My father was there too, watching a TV show about bass fishing.

"C'mon," I told Cody.

"No!"

"You don't got much choice in the matter," my father said. "Get going with your brother. And put some snap in your step."

Cody started to cry. "But I don't want to go, Daddy."

My father put his big hands on Cody's shoulders. "Sometimes you just gotta face the music. You'll feel better when it's over."

"I will not," Cody whimpered, but he followed me out the door anyway.

My brother shuffled his feet, walking as slow as humanly possible all the way to Kopsky's. I felt sorry for the kid. From the tragic look on his face you would have thought he was being dragged off to the guillotine.

"I don't wanna go," he kept moaning. "He's going to be so mad at me, Bobby."

"Maybe not," I said. "He might even appreciate that you're honest enough to admit what you did."

"He will not! He's gonna yell and scream. He's probably gonna hit me!"

I shook my head. "I won't let him do that."

That brought some temporary relief to Cody's face, but a moment later he looked miserable again. He halted on the sidewalk.

"I'm not going, Bobby. I'm staying here. *You* bring it back."

By now I'd just about run out of patience. I grabbed his hand and yanked him off the spot. "You're going to that store if I have to carry you there myself."

My brother was a total wreck, tears streaming down his face, by the time we entered the bead store at five thirty. I was nervous too. Even though I'd tried to reassure Cody, I honestly didn't know how Mr. Kopsky would react. The store was practically empty when we walked in. Kopsky was standing behind the counter, per usual, a toothpick between his teeth.

I cleared my throat.

"We came here," I began, "because of, well . . . it's about my little brother."

Cody had moved directly behind me. When I swung around to present my brother, Cody swung around too, hiding behind me. This happened three separate times, and it would have been funny if it wasn't so pathetic. I finally grabbed him and pulled him forward, front and center.

I handed him the paper bag. "Give it to Mr. Kopsky."

Without looking up, Cody placed the paper bag on the counter.

Mr. Kopsky picked up the bag and peered inside. He tilted it, allowing the necklace to slide into his big hands.

"He didn't pay for it," I explained.

I had a slim hope that Mr. Kopsky might nod, or show by his expression that he understood, but the look he gave Cody was a hard one. "He stole it, you mean."

Cody's eyes were fixed on the floor.

"Tell him," I urged.

My brother tried to speak, but no sound came out.

"Louder!" I ordered.

"Sorry," Cody said in a hoarse whisper. He didn't look up.

"He knows he did the wrong the thing, taking it without paying," I explained. "He—"

"You're the Steele kids, aren't you?" Kopsky said.

"Yeah."

Kopsky's upper lip curled back in a sneering smile.

"I know what your father did. I read all about him in the newspaper. Iron Steele."

I worked my jaw. "That has nothing to do with this."

"Oh, really?" Kopsky stared from Cody to me like we were repulsive things he had found stuck to the bottom of his shoe. "Give me one good reason why I shouldn't call the police."

At that word Cody rocked back; I could feel his whole body trembling.

I tried to work up a smile. "He's only five," I said lamely.

Kopsky glared. "Your daddy went to prison. Now your brother admits to robbing my store. I guess it runs in the family."

That's one thing about me. Push me; fine. Push me hard; I can handle it. But push me too far—watch out.

"Go outside," I told my brother. "Wait for me."

Cody didn't need any prodding. He vanished, banging the door behind him. Then it was just Kopsky and me. The smirk on his face made me sick to my stomach.

"You shouldn't talk to a little kid like that," I told him.

"How dare you lecture me!" Kopsky shouted. "Get out of my store! Get out or I will call the police!"

More than anything in the world I wanted to grab Kopsky by the shirt, pull him over the counter, and tune him up good. But that would have been disastrous. I knew that my only option was to leave. Reluctantly, I walked to the door.

"Don't you ever come back to this store!" he called after me.

ELEVEN

I RAN FIVE MILES THAT NIGHT. IT WAS A HAZY EVENING, BUT even so, I could still look up from the pavement to see the Whitestone buildings glowing on the hill.

Haven't you ever wanted something real bad even though you know you can't have it?

It was easy to pick out the rounded dome of the planetarium that had just been built. That, in a nutshell, showed the difference between Whitestone Prep and Riverview High School. They had just completed construction on a twenty-five-million-dollar, state-of-the-art planetarium. We couldn't even get our parking lot repaved.

Later I stuck my head back into the book I was reading, *One Flew Over the Cuckoo's Nest.* My favorite character was Chief Broom, the big Indian guy who never speaks to anyone in the mental hospital so people assume he's stupid. He has plenty of deep thoughts in his head, but he keeps them hidden. Everybody in the hospital thinks that Chief Broom can't talk—everybody but Randle McMurphy. Only McMurphy understands that Chief Broom isn't some kind of retard. McMurphy knows how strong the big Indian really is. He keeps encouraging him to bust out of that hospital, get away from Nurse Ratched, but Chief Broom doesn't leave. I guess he's too afraid.

I read for as long as I could, but when the words started swimming I snapped off the light and closed my eyes. Usually a long run left me so tired I'd fall asleep within minutes. But sometimes it worked in reverse. All that exercise and fresh air jacked me up like caffeine, and I'd lie in bed wide awake.

That's what happened now. I started thinking about Mom. Her cooking. The way she could take bad things and turn them into good. Like she'd take a bunch of limp vegetables and somehow whip them into an amazing stir-fry. Or if the milk in the refrigerator was sour, no problem: she'd use it to make hermit cookies with molasses and raisins.

Thinking about Mom always dredged up sadness, so I jumped from her to other people. My father. Cody. Mr. Kopsky.

I guess it runs in the family.

That smug look on his face put a bad taste in my mouth. To rinse it out, I thought about that tall blond Whitestone girl.

One person I tried *not* to think about was Rowan Pohi.

Inventing him had been fun at first, but picturing his grave in that empty city lot made me feel unexpectedly sad, so I pushed him from my mind.

My thoughts circled back to *One Flew Over the Cuckoo's Nest.* It hit me that Big Poobs was kind of like Chief Broom: both of them looked like big dumb guys, only they weren't. Poobs really was a smart kid, even if he didn't necessarily know it himself.

Sometimes I felt like Chief Broom too. Bottled up. Stuck with the wrong parent in a cramped apartment with a little brother who was convinced he was a full-blooded Native American. About to enter tenth grade in what was probably the worst high school in the city, or close to it. They say you're not supposed to feel sorry for yourself, but some nights I couldn't help it. I felt trapped, like one of those houseflies Turf liked to catch and hold, alive but doomed, in her mouth. I wanted to bust out too, but I didn't know how.

Next afternoon I met Marcus and Big Poobs at the IHOP. School would be starting in less than a week, and none of us was looking forward to it. We drank our sodas and talked about girls, movies, money, video games, then girls again.

"Think Rowan Pohi had a girlfriend?" Big Poobs asked, leaning back in the booth.

"Are you kidding?" Marcus replied. "Chicks were all over him."

"I had a dream about Rowan," Big Poobs said.

"You did?" I said.

Big Poobs nodded.

"What did he look like?" Marcus asked curiously.

"Straight brown hair," Poobs said, trying to remember. "He was taller than I expected. About six two."

For a minute, nobody said anything.

"Rowan Pohi was a freak," Marcus declared.

I shook my head. "No, he wasn't. He was like a regular kid."

"Think about it," Marcus continued. "He came into the world in a freakish way. And it was a freak illness that took him out."

I groaned. "Don't bring that up again."

I was bored all week, and by Saturday night I was going nuts. Poobs was working a double shift at Vinny's. Marcus was in Vermont visiting his father. By nine o'clock I felt like I would explode if I stayed in that apartment one minute longer, so I decided to go out for a run. My father appeared at my bedroom door just as I was lacing up my shoes.

"You going running now?"

"Yeah, why?"

He shrugged. "It's awful late."

That surprised me. These days my father mostly let me do whatever I wanted; it was unusual for him to comment on my plans, one way or another.

"There are streetlights the whole way," I said. "It's totally safe."

"Here." He tossed me something; I caught it in the air. "Put that around your wrist."

It was a small light attached to a strap.

"Where'd you get this?"

"Universal Sports."

"You bought it for me?"

He shrugged. "Wasn't expensive."

I looked down. "Well, uh, thanks."

"Be careful," he said. "There are plenty of knuckleheads driving around out there."

The wrist-light was perfect. It weighed next to nothing, so I barely noticed it while I ran. I tried to imagine my father going into Universal Sports, picking it up from the shelf, and paying for it at the checkout counter, but the picture didn't come into focus easily. I couldn't remember the last time he just went out and bought me something.

The weather was a perfect 72 degrees. I felt great, locked-in but loose, and decided to sprint the last quarter mile. I ran full bore until my quads burned and my heart was hammering in my chest. Still I kept going. I sprinted four long blocks, and I would have gone two blocks more except a red light forced me to stop. I stood on the sidewalk, hunched over, catching my breath while the sweat trickled down my upper back. As I was wiping my forehead I happened to glance up at the street sign.

Sibberson.

I felt an unexpected tug inside me.

Isn't life weird? We truly think that we are the ones making plans. We are convinced that we are making the important decisions in our lives. But maybe not. Maybe other forces are at work to make us do this or that.

Like now. I was supposed to follow my regular route home. But standing at the street corner, I felt a definite crosscurrent pulling me hard right. When the light changed to green, I hesitated. Before I realized what was happening, I found myself on Sibberson, fast-walking toward Spence.

The sky was dark by the time I reached the abandoned lot; I was glad I had the wrist-light.

What was I doing there? Why was I standing at that lonesome spot where Rowan was buried? To bear witness? Pay my respects?

I didn't know. I simply stood there, breathing, holding on to the chainlink fence and staring into that dark lot.

Goodbye, Rowan.

And that was it. I got a feeling of peace, like now it really was finished and I could go on with my life. *Closure:* isn't that the word? I was glad I'd come. I turned to leave, but as I did, a small noise reached my ears.

Pffff. Puffff. Pfff-pffff.

Rain. The first droplets were fat. Each one made a soft, distinct sound as it struck the dust. *Pfff-pufff. Puffff. Piffff.* The sound paralyzed me; I stood frozen to the spot. The rain started falling harder, until soon all those separate *pffffs* combined into one ragged noise that grew louder and louder still, like when you're making popcorn and it builds to the point when suddenly all the kernels are popping at the same time.

I was still standing outside the fence. Honestly, I hadn't planned on going any closer. But now I realized that rain would penetrate the few inches of dirt on that shallow grave, would soak through Rowan's papers. The ink would blur. All those words—*Congratulations, Rowan!*—would become unreadable and be lost forever.

I couldn't let that happen.

It was easy to find the opening in the fence. Looking around to make sure nobody was watching, I slipped underneath and moved toward the grave. Although there wasn't anybody around, I moved like an assassin, trying not to make the slightest sound.

Using the narrow flashlight beam, I located the three letters in the dirt.

RIP

The letters were already starting to blur.

I knelt down, pressing my knees into the earth. The rain on my neck felt warm, but I shivered. The nerves in my body jangled like a zillion tiny bells. I wondered what Marcus and Big Poobs would think about what I was doing. They'd either clobber me or laugh like crazy, and I wouldn't blame them either way, but it was too late to turn back now.

I pressed my right hand onto the moist dirt and dug down until my fingers located the two envelopes. I pulled them from the earth and repacked the dirt, taking care to make the spot look undisturbed. With my pinkie finger, I carefully retraced Rowan's initials on top of the grave.

I stood up and brushed away the dirt clinging to my bare knees. A moment later I was back under the fence. I tucked Rowan's envelopes into my shorts, pulled my shirt over them to keep the paper dry, and sprinted home through the pouring rain.

TWELVE

NEXT MORNING I WAS STARVING WHEN I WOKE UP. THERE wasn't much food in the house, so I decided to go buy some bagels.

The city air had a fresh, rain-washed smell when I stepped onto the sidewalk and headed toward Finagle A Bagel. A half dozen was our usual order: two chocolate chip for Cody, two onion for my father, and two everything for me.

"Hey there."

I swiveled around and—ba-boom!—there she was. The tall Whitestone girl I had been noticing on and off the last few weeks.

"Hi."

"Hey."

She stood in front of me like a study in whiteness: white T-shirt, white shorts, white teeth, blond hair. And long legs.

She extended her hand. "I'm Heather. Heather Reardon."

"Hi."

Awkwardly, I took her hand and shook it. She was tall for a girl; we stood eye to eye, and I'm close to six feet.

Heather grinned. "Well? What's your name?"

I met her grin, and raised her one.

"I'm Rowan," I said. "Rowan Pohi."

THIRTEEN

"I SWEAR, BOBBY," MOM SAID TO ME ONCE, "YOU MUST HAVE
been born on Opposite Day. Every time I expect you to do one
thing, you do the exact opposite. How on earth did you become
so impulsive?" She said this after I decided to go out for the
volleyball team even though I had never played volleyball in my
entire life.

I looked up *impulsive* in the dictionary. It means "spontane-
ous, reckless." Doing something without thinking it through. I
guess she was right. It was definitely an impulsive decision to
become Rowan Pohi.

Now we stood on the sidewalk, Heather Reardon and me,
blinking in the sunlight.

"I keep seeing you around." I gave her a mock-suspicious
look. "You aren't some kind of stalker, are you?"

She laughed out loud. "No, I swear!"

"Where do you live?" I asked.

"I live over on the Heights."

I nodded. "I sort of figured that."

There was an empty wooden bench, so we sat down.

"So what are you doing on this side of town?" I asked.

"I'm doing music camp at Salve Regina," she explained. "This is the last day."

"You play . . . ?" I pointed at the instrument case she was carrying.

"Saxophone."

"But that's a guy instrument, isn't it?"

"Hey!" She lightly smacked me on the shoulder; I took this as a promising sign.

I rubbed my shoulder, like I was mortally injured. "You go to Whitestone. I've seen you wearing the Stony T-shirt."

She gave me a demure smile. "I'm glad you're paying attention. How about you? Where do you go to school?"

"Same," I said casually.

Her face flooded with amazement. "You go to Whitestone?"

"Well, I got accepted there." I leaned back on the bench and let out a sigh. "I don't know if my family can swing the money. That school isn't exactly cheap."

"They have financial aid," she pointed out. "Your parents just have to fill out some forms."

"Yeah," I said. Thinking: *That ain't gonna happen.*

Heather crossed her long legs; I tried hard not to stare at them.

"Tomorrow's new-student orientation for the tenth-graders," she said. "The high school is grade ten through twelve, so all the students are new, technically, but most of us are coming from Whitestone Middle. So by now we're kind of used to the Whitestone way of doing things."

"Uh-huh."

"Anyway, I'm sure they'll have somebody from financial aid you can talk to."

"What time are we supposed to be there?" I asked casually.

"Nine o'clock. I guess I'll see you there."

"I guess you will."

She regarded me closely. "Did you grow up around here?"

I shook my head. "I moved here from Arizona at the beginning of the summer. I lived way out in the desert, little town named Piñon."

She smiled. "Wow, the Arizona desert. You must have been surrounded by cactuses."

"You mean cacti," I playfully corrected her.

"Righto." She glanced at her watch and sprang up. "Oops, gotta go or I'll be late to camp. See you tomorrow, Rowan!"

"Bye, Heather."

She waved and took two steps away, but then whirled around and took two steps back.

"Sit with me at lunch, okay?"

"You got it," I told her.

When Heather left for the second time, I was thinking she looked fine coming toward me and just as fine walking away.

I felt cranked up, wired. I went into the store and bought six bagels, plus the Sunday newspaper for my father.

After that I didn't go home like I'd planned; I guess it really was Opposite Day. I made a right and headed toward Kopsky's Gifts and Novelties. I had some unfinished business there.

This time the store was full of customers. Mr. Kopsky was at his regular perch behind the counter. The man did not look happy to see me.

"Didn't I tell you not to come in my store?"

I held up my hand, palm out. "I want to buy it."

His dark eyes flashed. "Buy what?"

"The Indian necklace." My voice was strong and steady. "I've got the money."

I don't want your money—that's what I feared he might say, and that would have shut me up. I was counting on his being a treasure troll, the greedy kind of guy who would never under any circumstances say no to money.

Kopsky stared at me, considering.

"That necklace costs a hundred and eight dollars, with the tax," he finally said.

"I'll take it."

While he went to get the necklace, I counted out five twenties and a ten. Kopsky took my money and counted it, twice. Then he made a show of carefully marking each bill with a black felt-tip marker, to make sure they weren't counterfeit, I guess. Reluctantly, he slid the necklace plus the two dollars' change across the counter to me.

"I need a bag."

Without speaking, Kopsky handed me a plastic bag. I put the necklace in the bag, tucked the bag in a pocket section of my cargo shorts, and left.

Buying that Indian necklace on top of the bagels and the Sunday newspaper had completely emptied my wallet. But I was whistling as I walked home.

FOURTEEN

NEXT MORNING I TOOK THE NUMBER 6 CROSSTOWN BUS and transferred to the number 1. The closer we got to Whitestone, the more kids my age got onto the bus. They must have been new students too, but many of them had found a way to buy Whitestone threads ahead of time, and most seemed to know each other. I hunkered down in my seat, wearing my black hoodie. I had a nervous stomach and my heart was racing, but I closed my eyes, pretending to sleep.

"There it is," a girl murmured.

Raising my head, I spotted the gold Whitestone lettering over a tall iron gate. I had seen the entrance a few times before, driving past with Mom. Beyond the gate a sweet-looking campus appeared, with sweeping lawns and half a dozen separate buildings. You could easily mistake it for a college if you didn't know better.

Getting off the bus, we were greeted by a student who looked like she might be Indian or maybe Pakistani. "New-student orientation is inside the union," she said, pointing at a building with ivy snaking up the side.

I followed twenty other new students along a diagonal walkway. Hard to believe that so much velvety grass, so many perfectly trimmed bushes and shrubs, could be found in such a grungy city as ours. It was like walking through a park. We entered the building marked UNION and stepped into a foyer dominated by a huge white fountain carved out of solid marble. Craning my neck, I gazed up at the dome ceiling overhead.

We passed through the lobby into a larger room where a woman with a clipboard was checking in the students. She flashed me a smile.

"And you are . . . ?"

"Rowan Pohi."

I tried to force myself to breathe normally while I waited for her to find the name on her list.

"There you are, Rowan. Do you have your preregistration card?"

"Uh-huh." I handed it to her.

"Excellent. If you step over there, you can get your Whitestone ID. It shouldn't take too long."

I stood in the short line, trying to stay calm.

I did it, I said to myself. *I'm inside the belly of the beast.*

While I waited, I checked out the other students. Only about half of them were wearing Whitestone clothing. This included the girl in front of me, who had shoulder-length dark hair. She caught my eye and zipped me a small, tight smile. I smiled back.

"There's something extremely . . . awkward about the first day of school, don't you think?" she asked.

"True," I admitted. "But we're all in the same boat."

"I'm trying not to feel seasick," she quipped.

"Didn't you go to Whitestone Middle School?"

She shook her head. "No, I went to Holy Sisters of Mercy. This place feels much different. I'm Robin, by the way. Robin Whaley."

"Rowan." I smiled. "Hey, they could make, like, a reality TV show about us. Robin and Rowan."

"Catchy," she admitted. "But it wouldn't be very juicy, at least my part of it."

I gave her a sleepy grin. "I'm not buying that."

"Next!"

A young man motioned for me to sit in front of the camera.

"Smile, Rowan."

Flash. Three minutes later I was holding an official White-stone ID card for Rowan Pohi. With my own mug. If only Marcus and Big Poobs could see me now. I got a funny pang thinking of my two buddies—guilt? regret?—but pushed it out of my mind. I'd have to deal with that later.

"Let me see."

Heather Reardon came out of nowhere and playfully yanked the ID out of my hands. She was wearing white shorts and a neon blue T-shirt that said ASK ME.

"Hi there." I was glad to see one familiar face.

"Hell-oooo." She peered at the ID card. "Very handsome."

I pointed at her shirt. "Can I ask you a question?"

She put her hands on her hips. "Shoot."

"What is the meaning of life?"

Heather laughed and grabbed my hand. "They've got dough-nuts to die for, but they're going fast. C'mon."

I waved at Robin as Heather led me to the refreshment table. There I helped myself to two doughnuts thickly crusted with sugar. Yum.

"The upper school is grade ten through twelve, just over a thousand students," Heather was saying. The room had sud-denly gotten noisy, so she had to stand close to me to be heard.

"Most of these kids went to Whitestone Middle, right?" I said. "So there already must be lots of cliques."

Heather shook her head. "Not really. There are three hun-dred fifty kids in the ninth grade class. And there are lots of new kids coming in from other schools, states, even other countries. Don't worry about it. This will be a whole new game for all of us."

Most of the kids around me were rocking the green Whitestone T-shirt. With my black Bob Marley T-shirt, I stood out like a sore thumb.

"I feel sort of . . . underdressed," I told Heather.

"No worries. Uniforms are optional this week."

"Shouldn't they call it Greenstone?" I suggested. "Or at least make these shirts white?"

Heather regarded me with mock-serious eyes. "Don't make that joke again, Rowan. Ever."

"I won't," I promised.

She handed me a glossy Whitestone-at-a-Glance brochure. I skimmed the first paragraph:

- Named one of the top five preparatory high schools seven years in a row
- 1:5 teacher-student ratio
- Outstanding faculty
- Encourages student initiative and independent study
- 99 percent of Whitestone grads attend four-year colleges

"Read it carefully," Heather advised. Playfully, she wrinkled her nose at me. "I may have to quiz you later."

"Rowan Pohi."

A young woman had appeared and was looking around, and I realized she wanted me. She led me into a small room and motioned for me to take the seat on the other side of the table.

"I'm Melody Ryder," she began. "Welcome to Whitestone, Rowan."

"Thank you."

She seemed no older than twenty-five, maybe even younger. Her dark brown hair was cut short and curled forward on the sides.

"Mrs. Ryder," I remembered. "You're the one who sent me the letter."

"*Ms.* Ryder," she corrected me. She wasn't wearing any wedding ring. "Yes, I'm director of admissions here at Whitestone."

How should I act? I wanted to seem confident, like I belonged in this school. But a new student at Whitestone would most likely be nervous, or at least shy, wouldn't he?

"Hmm, Pohi is an interesting name," she began. "Is that Native American?"

I shrugged. "Uh, possibly. My mother thinks there may be some Native American blood in the family, but we're not a hundred percent sure."

She lifted a piece of paper. With a start I realized it was the original application, the very same one that we filled out that fateful day at the IHOP. I tried not to stare at the darkish stain on the lower right, remembering exactly how it happened, Big Poobs accidentally dribbling pancake syrup. For a split second, my confidence wavered.

What the hell am I doing here?

"We're going to need it as soon as possible," Melody was saying.

"What?"

"Your high school transcript," she explained. "Your old high school hasn't sent it to us yet, and we really do need it. Would it help if I gave them a call?"

I swallowed. "No, that's okay. I'll call them."

"All right. Hopefully they'll send it right along. And you never gave us your phone number."

"Uh, our home phone has been disconnected," I said, stalling.

"Do you have a cell phone number?" she asked.

I gave it to her and watched her write it down. Then she studied the application. "You had a three point six grade point average—that's impressive."

"It would have been even higher," I put in, "except I took a pre-calculus course that was, like, impossible."

She smiled sympathetically. "I'm not much of a math person either. I see that you played football in Arizona. Your football coach sent a glowing letter of recommendation."

I nodded. "Coach García is the man."

"Is Piñon down by Phoenix or in the northern part of the state?" Ms. Ryder asked.

A stab of panic.

"I'm terrible on geography," I admitted. "We only lived there a few years."

"Well, I know Piñon is desert," she said. "It must have been hot during some of your football practices."

"Like an oven," I agreed.

"We have an excellent football team here at Whitestone. Are you planning on going out for the team?"

"I'm considering it. Yeah, definitely."

"I see you were National Honor Society, Rowan. What sorts of activities did you do?"

I blanked. Activities? I figured the National Honor Society was just a bunch of kids with high grades sitting around telling each other how smart they were. Ms. Ryder was waiting, so I had to make up something, quick.

"We did pancake breakfasts," I blurted. "To raise money. To, you know, buy books for some of the underprivileged kids in the area."

"That's wonderful."

She put down the application and briskly rubbed her hands together. "I'll help you fill out your class schedule, Rowan. But before I do, you must have some questions for me."

"Ah, um, I d-don't know," I stammered. Questions? "Well, yes, there is one thing. How about school uniforms? I know the school has a dress code."

She handed me a slip of paper. "This will tell you exactly what you need. You can get everything at the school store, which is in the union building."

I stared at the list: two green jerseys, khaki slacks, white shirt, blue tie, blue blazer, school sweatshirt, school athletic shorts, and T-shirt. This stuff would cost a small fortune.

"I didn't bring any money."

"Don't worry, you can bring a check on Wednesday." She smiled again, flashing perfect teeth. "Wednesday is the first day of school." She cleared her throat. "Now, as to the matter of tuition and fees. Will you be applying for financial aid?"

I nodded. "Probably."

"Then please follow me."

Ms. Ryder led me to the office of Jon Throckmorton, the man who ran the financial aid office at Whitestone. Throckmorton had thick wrists and pale blue eyes; his hair was cut in a military flattop. The dude was ripped.

"Hello, Rowan," he said, motioning me to take a seat. He

slid a thick packet over to me. "Your parents have to fill that out, okay?"

I glanced at the packet but didn't touch it.

"That, uh, might not be possible," I managed.

"Why not?"

"I live with my father, and, well, he can get kind of crazy."

His eyes narrowed. "Crazy?"

I nodded. "My father's got a wicked temper. He's got anger-management problems, seriously. Sometimes when I ask him the simplest question he flips out on me."

Throckmorton rolled up his sleeves to reveal lethal forearms. You would not want to meet this guy in a dark alley. "Well, someone has to fill out these forms. Your father, your mother, or your guardian, if you have one."

"My father won't," I insisted. "And my mother doesn't live with us."

"I don't know what to tell you, Rowan." Throckmorton folded his arms. "This school may have lofty goals, but at the same time, we all have to live in the real world. An education at a school like Whitestone is very expensive. Somebody has to pay for it. Otherwise we'd go broke. Understand?"

I nodded.

"You've got a couple of options." Throckmorton raised three blunt fingers, one after the other. "Your parents can write a check.

If they fill out these forms, you might be able to get financial aid from our office. Or you might win a scholarship."

I blinked. "Scholarship?"

"Yes, we do have a limited number of scholarships endowed by wealthy benefactors," he explained. "They're extremely competitive."

"What kind of scholarships?"

"They're all different." Throckmorton picked up a slender white folder and opened it. "Let's see. Here's one for a promising science student. This one is for 'exceptional aptitude in music.' One is for theater. Have you done much acting?"

"No." Except now.

"There's one for excellence in writing," Throckmorton said.

"I am a pretty good writer," I blurted out.

He regarded me closely. "You'll have to give a writing sample. Five hundred words."

"Okay." That didn't seem too hard. "When would I do the writing?"

"You can do it right now."

THROCKMORTON LED ME TO A TINY ROOM WITH A CHAIR, A desk, and one exam booklet. He said I would have up to forty-five minutes to write the essay. After he left, I opened the booklet and read what was printed on top of the first page.

What do you consider to be your greatest personal strength? What impact has this strength had on your life? (Note: Essay must be at least 450 words.)

Staring at those sentences, it hit me that the whole Whitestone adventure would not have gotten this far without my complete disregard of how the real world works, plus luck, plus guts. I was winging it, pure and simple, and I couldn't back off now. If I did, everything I had done to this point, every chance I'd taken, would be wasted. It would be a miracle if I could win this writing scholarship. To do so, I'd have to write an awesome essay. Nothing less would do.

It has been said that a person's strength is also their weakness, two sides of the same coin. Elvis Presley and Michael Jackson were phenomenal performers, but in the end they became performers in their own lives. Like Icarus, they flew too close to the sun. The bright lights of celebrity melted their wings.

I'm no Elvis (and definitely no Michael Jackson) but I realize the same thing is true in my life. My strength is also my weakness. I am an impulsive person. The dictionary defines this word as "not thinking something all the way through." This part of my character has gotten me into trouble, for instance when I was four and thought my crayons felt too cold so I put them on a radiator to warm them up. My parents were not very happy to see our radiator decorated with rainbow streams of melted wax.

But being impulsive has its upside, too. I have never been afraid to reach for the golden ring. That's part of my personal philosophy. I'm a fighter. I believe that if you want something, you have to go for it. Period.

When I think of the term "personal strength"

the thing that comes to my mind is something I once read about a Native American tribe (the Navajos, I think). This tribe had fierce and fearless warriors. Those men had a unique and peculiar way of stalking their enemies. On noiseless feet they would sneak up close to their foes. They would shrink the distance, moving closer and closer, until they were so close they could hear the sleeping breath of the enemy warrior. Close enough to feel the heat of his blood.

At this distance a warrior could easily kill his foe, but he does not. Instead he reaches forward and taps his enemy on the shoulder. Then, before his "victim" realizes what just happened, the attacking warrior disappears into the forest. The message is clear: I got to you. I could have ended your life, but I didn't. I had the stealth and I had the strength, but I didn't have to use it.

Imagine this from the victim's point of view. He is awoken from a sound sleep to find his mortal enemy has touched him gently on the arm. What could be more demoralizing? After having his life spared in this way, the warrior would return home in shame and defeat.

This story made a lasting impression on me. It represents the kind of personal strength I admire most — having plenty of power in reserve, but only using that power if forced to do so, with no other choice.

I finished writing and signed the bottom of the sheet—Rowan Pohi—putting a bold dot above the final *i*. Next I counted words—not quite 450, so I went back and inserted a few more adjectives. I reread the essay. I still had plenty of time left, so I read it again. The phrase *the heat of his blood* worried me a little—too violent?—but in the end I decided to leave it in. There would be essays from other kids trying to win this scholarship. I needed strong images that readers wouldn't easily forget.

I stepped out of the test room and handed the booklet to Throckmorton, who was sitting at his desk.

"How did you do?" he asked.

I shrugged. "Okay. I hope you like it."

"I'm not one of the readers," he said. "We have a team of people who score the essays."

I nodded. "You remind me of my junior high football coach."

For the first time, Throckmorton managed a smile. "As a matter of fact, I am the football coach here at Whitestone."

"Oh."

He peered up at me. "Plan on trying out for the team?"

"Maybe. I played wide receiver."

"Are you fast?"

"Yeah," I admitted.

Throckmorton gave me a thoughtful look. "First practice is Wednesday. Bring your cleats. We'll see what you've got, Rowan."

SIXTEEN

THAT MORNING PASSED IN A BLUR; BY LUNCHTIME I WAS
starving. The lunchroom was already packed when I got there.
I put my tray down on the empty end of a table and started to
eat. Luckily, I didn't mind eating alone. The food was delicious,
a major upgrade from the stuff they tried to give us at Riverview. I had a tasty pulled-pork sandwich with french fries that
were crispy and hot.

After lunch they divided the kids into two groups for a tour
of Whitestone. I got assigned to Ms. Ryder's group. She showed
us the huge library with a dozen skylights, three different gym-
nasiums, an Olympic-size pool, a state-of-the-art weight room,
even a rifle range. The football field had brand-new synthetic
turf, the expensive kind that feels exactly like natural grass. I
was dying to see the planetarium, but Ms. Ryder said they were

doing last-minute work on the lighting, and it wouldn't be open until later in the week.

At the end of the day there was a reception in the library with Dr. Paul LeClerc, the headmaster. I carefully printed ROWAN POHI on my blank nametag and poured myself a glass of punch. LeClerc worked the room like a politician, making sure to shake hands with every new student. On long tables they had silver trays overflowing with fresh fruit and cheese squares skewered by colorful toothpicks. No way they would ever have a reception like this at Riverview. I found a basket overflowing with individually wrapped Lindt chocolate balls; I stashed a few in my pocket for later.

At three o'clock I boarded the bus. The other new students got off, one by one, until the last one stepped onto the sidewalk and I was the only kid left on the bus.

I leaned forward, letting my face fall into my hands. My head was swimming. I felt exhausted, discombobulated, but all jacked up too. I sat there, taking deep breaths, as I changed back from Rowan Pohi to Bobby Steele.

My phone beeped—a text message from Marcus.

Whr r u?

Marcus and Big Poobs! I felt a stab of crushing guilt so intense I had to close my eyes to ride it out. My buddies should have been part of this. I should have told them what I was doing, without a doubt. So why hadn't I?

Because I would have had to tell them that I dug up Rowan's grave.

Because I would have had to swear them to secrecy, which would have put them in an awkward position.

Because if they mentioned it to anyone else, I'd be sunk.

Because I was one selfish asshole.

Marcus: Whr r u dude?

Me: #1 bus

Marcus: Can u hang? me and poobs r bored

Me: IHOP in 20?

Marcus: Yessir

Me: brng $

Marcus: Duh

Me: Can I borrow 100? Ask Poobs too

Marcus: 50 each?

Me: 100 each f u v it

Marcus: Yow   dunno

Me: I need it

When I arrived, Marcus and Big Poobs were already waiting in our regular booth on the street side.

"I ordered you a root beer," Marcus said as I sat down.

"Power straws!" Poobs cried.

Power straws was a tradition we started back when we were ten years old. As a ritual, it was silly beyond belief, but we still did it when the three of us met up. Ripping the paper off our straws, we leaned in and held the tips together, pretending we were some kind of space warriors crossing three intensely charged molecular beams. Poobs supplied the *zzzzzzzzzzzzzzzz-sssstttt* sound effects.

The waitress brought our drinks and I took a pull of soda.

"So what gives, mystery boy?" Marcus asked.

"Wait a sec," I said. I must have drunk too fast because my head began to throb.

Marcus studied me curiously. "What were you doing on the number one bus? That's the wrong side of town."

I looked from Marcus to Big Poobs, not sure what to say.

"Hel-lo," Marcus said. "Anybody home?"

I tried to find a way to explain. "Look, we're friends, right?"

They nodded.

"I mean good friends. 'Really good friends.' " I was using air quotes. "And once in a while 'really good friends' have to forgive other 'really good friends' for something they might have done. Right?"

Marcus stared at Big Poobs. "I have no idea what he's talking about. Do you?"

"Nope," Poobs admitted. "You're coming in kinda fuzzy, Bobby."

I drummed the table, trying to think of another approach.

"Stony invasion," Marcus reported.

Four kids with Whitestone sweatshirts climbed into a booth against the wall. I thought I recognized one kid from the new-student orientation and sank down in my seat so he wouldn't see me.

"They're everywhere," Poobs muttered.

Marcus swiveled around and gave me an expectant look. "So?"

His high-pitched voice reminded me of the time when we were much younger and he'd invited me to his birthday party but I'd forgotten to tell him if I could come. In school he'd asked the same question—So?—in the same tone and with the same expression as he did now. I felt something give way inside me.

"I was coming back from school."

Marcus smelled a rat. "School doesn't start till Wednesday. What school?"

Softly, I uttered the name: "Whitestone."

Poobs's eyebrows jumped a foot. "What were you doing there?"

"Today was new-student day."

Marcus smiled. "Oh. You going to Whitestone now?"

"Yeah." I nodded, like it was no big deal. "Well, technically, Rowan Pohi is going to Whitestone."

For a long moment, nobody spoke. It dawned on them both at the exact same moment.

"You're . . . Rowan Pohi?" Big Poobs whispered.

I nodded. "Yeah."

Marcus was thunderstruck. "*You* turned into *him?*"

"Yeah. I guess so."

"But how . . . since when?" Big Poobs sputtered.

"A couple days ago," I said.

I don't think they would have been any more flabbergasted if I'd told them I was six months pregnant.

"You really went to the school?" Marcus demanded. "What about those papers? Weren't you supposed to bring them with you?"

"I did."

"But . . . how?"

"I dug up the grave."

They stared at me hard. Marcus shook his head. Big Poobs flat-out refused to believe it. "No, you didn't. You wouldn't."

"Yes, I did."

"You dug up his *grave?*" Marcus repeated in disbelief. "That's, like, sacrilegious."

I winced. "I know. Sorry."

Big Poobs was dazed. "Rowan rose from the dead? Only Jesus and vampires do that."

I smiled. "Only you would put Jesus and vampires in the same sentence."

But Marcus wasn't smiling. He looked angry. Hurt. "Why didn't you tell us?"

Why hadn't I told them? "Because you—"

Marcus interrupted: "Because you had to keep us on a— what do they call it?—a need-to-know basis. Huh? Is that it?"

"Listen, I—"

Marcus turned away, facing the street. "You really suck, man."

It was true, but I had to defend myself anyway.

"I wasn't trying to freeze you out," I countered. "Look, I only went one day. I'm telling you now, aren't I?"

"You are un-be-lievable," Marcus snarled. "You're really going to transfer to Whitestone?"

"Yeah," I admitted. "I already have."

"But it's a private school," Big Poobs pointed out. "Since when does your father have that kind of money?"

"Rowan's trying to get a scholarship," I explained.

Marcus stared. "Rowan? Or you?"

"Both. We're kind of a package deal." I tried to laugh but couldn't make it sound right.

Marcus shook his head. "Oh, I see, Mr. Multiple Personality."

Long pause. We slurped the dregs of our drinks.

"What's it like inside Whitestone?" Poobs asked curiously.

"Pretty slick," I told him. "The football field is, like, professional. All the equipment in the weight room looks brand-new. They had this, like, reception with little cheese cubes and fancy cookies and chocolate."

I took the Lindt chocolate balls out of my pocket and put them on the table. "Help yourself."

The way Marcus stared at those Lindt balls, I thought they might melt right there on the table. "You're a Stony now." His face was hard. "You're one of them."

"I am not!"

Marcus flashed me a nasty smile. "Oh no?"

"Look, I'm sorry, Marcus. I didn't plan it this way."

Marcus stood up. "I gotta go."

"Wait." I grabbed his shoulder. "Remember my text? I need some money."

Marcus opened his eyes wide in astonishment. "First you go and dig up Rowan's grave, and now you want my money. Is that how it goes?"

"I need to buy some clothes at the school store," I lamely explained. "They have a dress code at Whitestone."

"I brought a hundred," Big Poobs said, handing me a wad of bills.

Marcus dropped five twenties on the table and headed toward the door.

"I'll pay you back," I called after him.

"You're damn right you will," he said without turning around.

SEVENTEEN

THAT NIGHT I ALTERED MY ROUTE SO I COULD RUN PAST Riverview High School. The parking lot was an ugly construction site, ripped up and half finished, with piles of dirt and discarded coffee cups. Was it possible that I had spent my last day at that sorry school?

I felt bad about Marcus's reaction, but what could I do? Now that Rowan Pohi was up and running, well, I couldn't wuss out on him. The whole thing was still very shaky; I had to be committed two hundred percent. There were a zillion loose ends to figure out, like how to be at Whitestone on Thursday and work at my father's garage at the same time.

So I lied. I seemed to have gotten good at lying. I told my father that Big Poobs had gotten me a part-time gig busing tables at Vinny's on Thursday. Could I do those oil changes on Saturday? He said fine, just as long as the work got done and done right.

Cody was excited about his first day of school. He laid out his new school clothes the night before. Early Wednesday morning he came into my bedroom while it was still dark.

"Is it time for school, Bobby?"

My clock said 5:44 A.M. "No! It's way too early!"

"But I gotta go to school!"

My brother was completely dressed. He even had his backpack on.

"Go back to sleep!" I told him. "It's not time to wake up!"

"But I'm already dressed. I brushed my teeth!"

I took him to the den and made him lie down.

"I'll wake you up in an hour," I promised.

"I'm not tired!"

"Close your eyes." I covered him with a blanket and went back to bed.

My father drove Cody to school on the first day. I waved goodbye, then ran to catch the crosstown bus.

At school, I swiped Rowan's ID card; the front door clicked and allowed me to push through. At 7:35 there were only a few students milling around the halls. The first thing on my list was a visit to the Whitestone school store. The hallways were busy twenty minutes later when I emerged wearing a green shirt and khakis. I had stuffed my regular clothes in my backpack. I still needed to buy a blue blazer to the tune of ninety-five dollars, but I decided to wait until they assigned lockers so I'd have a place to hang it up.

Heather materialized as if out of thin air.

"Well, well, well, look who's rocking the Whitestone duds." She leaned back to admire me. "My, my. That shirt fits you perfectly."

"Yeah? Not too tight?"

She smiled. "Oh, no."

The day began with a school assembly. The place was full; almost everybody was wearing the green Whitestone T-shirt. Including me. I still couldn't wrap my head around the idea that I was a Stony. I felt almost dizzy, like I was floating in space. A dose of gravity, that's what I needed. But where to find it?

A minister got up to say a prayer. Then Melody Ryder introduced Dr. Paul LeClerc.

"Our motto at Whitestone Academy is Achievement and Integrity," he began. "Those are nonnegotiables around here."

I closed my eyes, letting LeClerc's voice wash over me. I tried to imagine this happening at Riverview—the kids all intently listening to this pompous speech—but the picture wouldn't come into focus.

After the assembly Heather and I filed outside to pick up our schedules. A dozen guidance counselors and other staff members, including Ms. Ryder, were on hand to answer questions or point kids in the right direction.

"Lemme see your schedule." Heather took it out of my hand. "Oh, no, we've only got biology together. I've got third lunch— you've got first." She looked indignant. "What's up with that?"

Robin Whaley pushed through the crowd, clutching her schedule.

"I'm glad to report that I've been assigned to Gryffindor," she announced breathlessly. "How about you, Rowan? Please don't tell me they put you in Hufflepuff."

Heather frowned. "Don't make that joke again. Ever."

"Sorry," Robin said sheepishly. "I've never been very good at small talk."

"What's your name?"

"Robin."

"I'm Heather. You didn't go to school here last year, did you?"

"No." Robin shook her head. "I was at Holy Sisters of Mercy."

"People say that's a real good school," Heather said, though she didn't sound like she believed it herself.

On the first day the school had a shortened schedule, with just enough time for teachers to introduce themselves.

"What do we do now?" I asked. "We've got a half-hour before first period."

"Dr. LeClerc said we could go see the planetarium," Robin said.

I shrugged. "Okay by me."

Robin turned to Heather. "Do you want to come along?"

"I've already seen it," Heather said with a dismissive wave. "But you guys should definitely check it out. Catch you later, Rowan."

The planetarium smelled brand-new. Robin took the seat next to me. Most of the other seats filled up with kids too. The seats tilted almost all the way back, so you could gaze straight up at the wide expanse where various stars and other celestial bodies would be projected. The cushy seats were unbelievably comfortable, and I felt my eyes beginning to close. It might be hard to stay awake in this room, especially in the dark with your seat tilted back.

"My name is Dr. Kokoris," a teacher began. He was in his late fifties, with a shock of white hair that made me think of Einstein. "Every day, in this room, I will create the universe and its galaxies in a manner not unlike God Himself."

The other kids giggled.

"What were God's first words?" Dr. Kokoris demanded.

To my horror, I realized that he was pointing directly at me.

"Ah, umm . . . 'Let there be light'?" I guessed.

Dr. Kokoris grinned. "This young man knows his Genesis! Yes, those were God's first four words: *Let there be light!* And those are the first words I will say every morning as we begin to explore celestial worlds. To do so, we will rely on powerful telescopes that will transport us billions of light-years away."

To this, a boy behind me cracked: "All the way to Uranus."

Someone laughed. Dr. Kokoris whirled around and glared suspiciously at me.

"This planetarium cost more than twenty-five million dollars, so you must take very good care of it," he declared. "You *will* take care of it, understand? No eating. No drinking. No chewing gum. No putting your feet up on another seat. No *breathing* without my permission."

More giggles.

"Remember: in this planetarium I am God, and I will find you," Dr. Kokoris concluded. He paused to clear his throat. "Now, let's take her out for a little spin, shall we?"

The room went dark. I tilted my seat back farther just as a tiny blue spot appeared on the black screen. It grew larger and larger until I could see it was the Earth. This was followed by an asteroid incinerating itself as it plummeted to Earth. Soon all sorts of weird nebulae, galaxies, white dwarfs, black holes, shooting stars were flashing across the expanse above us. It ended with some mind-boggling photos showing what Kokoris called star nurseries, or EGGs ("evaporating gaseous globules"), where new stars were being born.

"That Dr. Kokoris has a God complex," I muttered as we filed out.

Robin smiled. "If so, he's found the perfect job."

My first-period class was English. There were only fifteen students. I took a seat next to a tall kid with short, frosted hair. The English teacher introduced himself as Mr. Nardone.

"In tenth-grade English we will be reading and discussing lots of great literature," Nardone began. "We'll start the year with *To Kill a Mockingbird*."

The tall kid next to me glanced over and caught my eye.

"I read that book over the summer."

"Like it?" I whispered.

"Do you like Chinese water torture?" he replied.

After English I had Spanish, which was *much* harder than anything I'd had at Riverview. *Señor* Backman spoke in nothing but rapid Spanish; I understood about 10 percent of what he said. I was the only boy in the room. The class was jammed with nerdy girls who looked like they had nothing better to do every night than study for umpteen hours. For the first time, I got a sinking feeling, like I was in way over my head.

It was a relief to go from Spanish to biology. Heather Reardon sent me a wink from the far side of the room as Mr. Rasmussen passed out the syllabus. Biology seemed like it would be manageable. In fact, except for Spanish, the classes at Whitestone didn't seem like they'd be too hard, so long as I kept myself organized and didn't get behind in my assignments. Actually, the classes weren't much different from Riverview's except there were fewer kids in each class, and the teachers smiled more.

The chicken fingers they served for lunch were phenomenally tasty; I had to force myself not to eat too fast. The kids at the other end of the table all knew each other and chattered nonstop. I wondered how long it would take for me to make a few friends.

When the other kids got up to leave, I still wasn't done. As I was eating my final chicken finger, I became aware of two guys at a nearby table staring at me. I did my best to ignore them.

"You should avoid fried foods."

I glanced up to find that one of the kids who'd been staring at me was standing by my table. He was tall and wiry, with an earring and a spray of acne on his chin. Another boy stood behind him.

"I'm Seth. This is Brogan." He peered down skeptically. "Who be you?"

"Rowan."

"Yeah? Rowan what?"

"Rowan Pohi."

Seth grinned at Brogan. "Rowan Pohi."

Brogan nodded. "Nice."

"You from around here?" Seth asked.

I shook my head. "Nope. Arizona."

Seth turned to Brogan again. "Arizona!"

Brogan smiled. "Nice."

Seth snatched a french fry off my plate.

"Hey!"

"Oops, sorry," Seth said. "I honestly dunno why I did that. My mommy taught me it's wrong to steal."

It was eerie the way his voice lingered on that word *steal*. Now he leaned forward and brought his face close to mine.

"I've seen you before, Rowan Pohi."

Something kicked in my gut. "I doubt it."

"Oh, but I have." Seth gave me an unpleasant smile. "And you better be careful. Consider this my first warning."

He snatched another fry off the plate.

I jumped up. "You touch my food again, I'll shove my fist up your nose."

Wiggling his fingers in mock dread, Seth strolled away, with Brogan close behind.

EIGHTEEN

EIGHTEEN

I GOT A TEXT LATER THAT AFTERNOON WHILE I WAS UP IN MY bedroom reading the first pages of *To Kill a Mockingbird*.

How R U?

Heather. I was glad for the distraction, so I texted her back. A moment later my cell phone rang.

"What are you doing?" Heather asked.

"I'm reading *To Mock a Killingbird*, for English. Have you read it? It's brutal."

She giggled. "Hey, Rowan, remind me: what's that girl's name we were talking to this morning? Mona?"

"No, Robin," I said.

"Oh yeah. I'm going to buy that girl some smiley pills."

"I guess she is sort of solemn," I admitted, "but she seems okay."

Heather began telling me about the horse farm her family

owned in upstate New York. She described the horses, one by one, explaining their personalities in great detail.

"Onyx would be perfect for you to ride," she told me. "She's very cool. A real sweetheart. You'll fall in love with her."

I laughed nervously. "If I don't kill myself first."

"You'll be a natural," she insisted. "I can just tell."

At that moment my phone started beeping, low battery, so we had to say goodbye. After that, I plugged in my phone to re-charge it. I was surprised to see that we'd been talking for al-most an hour.

At supper that night I asked Cody how he liked kindergarten.

"It's pretty good, but not all the way awesome."

"How come?"

"You can't run outside—you have to walk real slow," he complained. "And you can't tackle kids on the playground."

"It's not summer camp," my father said gruffly. "The sooner you realize that, the better off you'll be."

Cody's face grew sad; for a second I thought he might start to cry. "Why are you being so mean, Daddy?"

"It's school," my father said. "It's not supposed to be all about fun and games—you're there to learn."

Lightly, I jabbed Cody on the shoulder. "You'll get used to it."

After we cleaned up the dishes, I started working on my Spanish homework. My phone began to vibrate. Another text message, this one from Big Poobs.

Poobs: U got marked absent

Me: ?

Poobs: They called yr name. Bobby Steele. RemMbR?

I texted back—LMAO—though I wasn't laughing.

The next morning brought a steady rain, so I got wet running from the bus stop into the school building. I made a mental note to buy one of those little fold-up umbrellas I could tuck in my backpack.

"Rowan!"

Ms. Ryder approached. She was cradling a cup of coffee.

"Good morning, Rowan. How have things been going?"

"Fine. Great."

"I'm glad to hear that, but I still haven't received transcripts from your previous high school."

"Oh, really?" I tried to think. "Yeah, well, nothing happens very fast in that part of Arizona."

"I know, but I really need those transcripts."

"I called the school," I told her. "The secretary promised she'd send them along in the next week or so."

She nodded. "Hopefully they'll send them soon."

My wet Whitestone shirt didn't dry as fast as I expected; I shivered through the first few periods. There was a quiz in English followed by another difficult Spanish class.

"Homework is on the board," *Señor* Backman reminded us as the bell rang. "*Señor* Pohi, *¿podría hablar con usted?*"

I glanced up. "Huh?"

"Could I please have a word with you?"

So I gathered my stuff and stopped at Backman's desk. He was a young guy, maybe thirty, with a shock of short black hair.

"You didn't say very much in class today, *Señor* Pohi."

"I know."

He tapped a pen on his desk. "You received the syllabus, didn't you? Half of your grade is based on class participation."

"I was a little lost today," I admitted.

"Maybe you're in the wrong class. Maybe you should be in Spanish One."

"I took Spanish One last year," I said. Which was true.

He blinked at me, not mercilessly, but not with a whole lot of sympathy either. "The language program here at Whitestone is probably a lot stronger than what you had at your previous school. You're going to have to show me you belong in this class. Right now I'm not convinced. *¿Entiende?*"

"*Sí,*" I replied.

Heather sat next to me in biology. The large room was divided into two parts: regular desks, and a lab area where we would be dissecting and doing other experiments. Mr. Rasmussen announced that the first unit would be on insects that mimic other insects. At Riverview, teachers spent half the period checking attendance, doing paperwork, and getting the class settled. The teachers at Whitestone didn't waste time like that; they all got right down to business.

Rasmussen began by showing a series of images: bees that mimic ants; beetles camouflaged to look like leaves; walking sticks; katydids; and several others.

"Why would insects mimic or imitate other insects?" Rasmussen asked, snapping on the lights. "I'll give you two minutes to think about that. Make a list of possible reasons why. Speculate. In science, a speculation is an educated guess. We will be doing a lot of scientific speculation in this class."

The class grew quiet.

"All right, let's see what you came up with," Rasmussen said exactly two minutes later. "Miss Reardon?"

"Competition for food and avoiding predators," she said. "I couldn't come up with anything else."

"That's a good start. How about you, Mr. . . . Pohi, isn't it?" He studied his class sheet. "Why might one insect want to mimic others of a different species?"

"Just to fit in," I said, which seemed obvious.

Rasmussen folded his arms. "Say more about that, Rowan."

"Well, it's like what she said about predators," I said. "You're either trying to eat them, or avoid being eaten by them, so if you can somehow trick them into thinking you're one of them, well, you have a better chance of surviving."

I was eerily aware that I was also talking about myself.

"It's like wearing a disguise," I continued. "You don't want to be different from the group. You want to fit in. If they knew you were different, it would be dangerous."

Rasmussen nodded. "What about sex?"

I felt the whole class staring. Why was he picking on me?

"What about it?" I finally managed.

Everybody laughed, including Heather. I wanted to laugh too, but I was too embarrassed.

Rasmussen smiled. "Could you speculate? Put yourself in their place. If you were an insect, what impact could mimicking another insect have on your sex life?"

I wasn't going near that one. I was relieved when he stepped back to address the class.

"For homework tonight, I'm giving you an article to read on this subject," Rasmussen said. "A very *steamy* article."

"I doubt that," Heather muttered.

Right before lunch I ran into Robin and told her what *Señor* Backman had said about maybe I didn't belong in Spanish Two.

She offered to help me with Spanish. We met in a small library conference room right after school. It was sealed-in and private, with windows looking out to the rest of the library. Robin began by quizzing me on verb tenses: present, past, conditional. It was the future that gave me the most trouble.

"I will go," she said.

"*Vamos a ir,*" I guessed.

She shook her head. "*Voy a ir. Vamos* is for *we.* Let's try another. How would you say *I will play?*"

I didn't really know, but I took a stab. "*Voy a leer.*"

"Wrong-o. *Voy a jugar.*" She frowned at me. "Rowan."

I winced. "I know, I know."

"You have to learn this stuff now or you'll get buried," she persisted. "Look at the verbs on pages a hundred and one and a hundred and two, and memorize them."

"Okay."

We worked for the next half-hour. Then, through the glass window, we saw a girl with long red hair stroll past. I don't think she realized we were looking at her. She stopped and lifted herself on tiptoes, searching for a book on the upper shelf. The girl was absurdly beautiful. Honestly, she could have been a model. I tried not to stare, especially with Robin sitting there.

Robin sighed. "It's hard being ordinary in a school with so many beauties walking around."

"Braces," I declared. "I'll bet you twenty bucks every one of these girls has had braces. That's the secret. Having perfect teeth helps a lot."

Her eyes were mournful. "It's a lot more than that."

"Anyway, who cares?" I smiled. "I don't mind. Being ordinary, I mean."

"I hate to break it to you, but you're not ordinary." She sounded testy. "You're a bit of a babe."

I tried not to blush. "I am not!"

"Oh yes you are. And don't try to act surprised. Good-looking people know they're good-looking. Always."

"I think you're good-looking," I said, hoping that didn't sound too lame or tacked-on.

"No, I'm not. I've got a way-too-big forehead. Not to mention my chunky legs. And just look at this drab hair." She motioned at the girl beyond the glass. "I'd *kill* for hair like that."

I pulled the window blinds, cutting off our view of the red-haired goddess who still had not located her book.

"I'm dorky-looking," Robin concluded.

"No, you're not," I murmured.

Our eyes locked. For a millisecond I thought about kissing her, right there in the conference room. Nobody would have seen. But it would have been a mercy kiss. Robin was nobody's fool—I doubted she would fall for it.

The moment passed. She glanced at her watch.

"I guess I better go. My mother's coming to pick me up."

"Thanks, Robin. I mean it—I owe you one."

"No, you don't." She closed the Spanish book. "Work on the future tense."

"I will," I promised. *"Lo haré."*

Robin smiled.

NINETEEN

THAT NIGHT I DREAMED I WAS IN THE PLANETARIUM WITH Robin. It was dark. When I turned to her, I found her leaning in for a kiss. But right at that moment, Robin's face morphed into Heather's. She kissed me, softly at first, then with an open mouth.

When I saw Heather the next morning I felt a little shy around her, as if something had actually happened between us. She looked nice in a white blouse with a charcoal-colored skirt. I noticed that most boys were wearing white shirts with the Whitestone blue blazer, which I had yet to buy.

"Guess we're supposed to be wearing blazers today, huh?"

"Yeah, they call it Formal Fridays, but it's optional this week."

"I better buy my blazer next week."

She made a sad face. "I was thinking we could hang out this weekend, Rowan, but we're going away to our horse farm."

"You would choose riding horses over hanging out with me?"

"Possibly," she admitted with a guilty grin. "But I have a plan."

"She has a plan," I declared to nobody in particular.

"On Monday we have early release for a teacher workshop. You want to come over my house? My parents won't be home."

"Definitely, sure."

"We've got a pool," she added coyly, "so bring your bathing suit."

The morning classes went fine. I'd taken Robin's advice and done extra verb work, so I did have an easier time in Spanish. At lunch I wolfed down three tacos. I was the last one left at the table, as before. And once again I became aware of those two kids staring at me. Seth and Brogan, the ones who had snatched french fries off my plate a few days ago. Like jackals in Africa, they moved closer, watching me finish my lunch. But if they were trying to intimidate me, it wasn't working.

"Why don't you guys go hassle someone else?" I suggested.

"No hassles," Seth promised with a formal bow. "We come in peace."

Ignoring them, I took a last leisurely bite of my taco.

"See, there's a terrible rumor going around," Seth said confidentially. "From what I heard, someone's trying to steal his way into this school."

My gut tightened.

"What do you think about that, Rowan Pohi?" Brogan asked.

I shrugged. "Doesn't concern me."

Now Seth took the seat directly across the table from me. He leaned forward and spoke in a low voice.

"I know who you are, dude. You're Bobby Steele."

I wiped my mouth with a napkin. "And you're Hannah Montana."

"Bobby Steele," Seth repeated.

I gave them a quizzical look. "I don't know what you're talking about. My name is Rowan—"

"Cut the Rowan crap, okay?" In a split second Seth's face changed, showing a hard side of him I hadn't seen before. "You know how I know who you are? *I was in your PE class at Riverview for two weeks before I transferred to Whitestone.* You were the fastest kid in class. They had the Pizza Challenge the second week of school. You came in first."

Stalling, I took a long drink of chocolate milk. Honestly, I wasn't sure what my next move was, or if I even had one.

"Well?" Seth demanded. "What do you think, Bobby?"

"You clowns should mind your own business. That's what I think."

Seth did not take his eyes off me. "I'm making this my business, Bobby boy."

"You are totally screwed," Brogan interjected.

"Wait, hold on, maybe not," Seth said, holding his hand up to Brogan. "There's one thing we could do."

I didn't see any choice but to sit and listen.

"I have this Aunt Millie," Seth continued. "She's real nice but real poor, you know? I was thinking if you maybe give me ten bucks a week, I could give it to Aunt Millie so she has enough to eat and pay her bills."

I smiled. "That sounds like blackmail."

Seth shook his head. "No, no, you got it all wrong. The money wouldn't be for us; it would be for Aunt Millie. To help her out."

I stared at him. "Let me get this straight. If I pay you ten bucks a week you'll forget all about Bobby Steele, huh? Do I really look that stupid?"

Now it was Seth's turn to smile. "That's not stupid. That's smart. That's what I call a win-win situation. A win for you and a win for, uh, Aunt Millie."

"Ten bucks a week is forty bucks a month," I pointed out. "That's four hundred eighty bucks a year."

"Bobby Steele is a math genius," Seth told Brogan.

Brogan giggled. Seth turned to me and pointed at the tall stained-glass windows in the lunchroom.

"Think about it, Bobby," he said. "You wouldn't want to lose all this, would you?"

Right then Heather appeared at the table.

"I sneaked out of study hall," she announced.

"Well, hello, hello," Seth murmured, slowly giving her the once-over.

Heather flashed him a murderous look. "Don't start with me, Seth." She turned to me. "What gives, Rowan? What did these toads say to you?"

"Nothing," I mumbled.

"Rowan!" Brogan cried. "She called him Rowan. Isn't that cute?"

Heather gave me a puzzled look. "What's going on?"

"We were just giving Bobby, uh, I mean Rowan, the inside scoop on Whitestone," Seth explained. "Ta-ta!"

They left. Heather took the adjacent chair and slid in close. I felt the side of her knee press against mine.

"Seth and Brogan are not nice people," she murmured. "They're evil. They weren't bullying you, were they?"

"Don't worry," I said. "I can take care of myself."

That afternoon I went to the football meeting. Once again I had that what-am-I-doing-here feeling, even more so after the little chat I'd had with Seth and Brogan. As much as I hated to admit it, Brogan was right.

I was totally and royally screwed.

I counted fifty-one guys at the meeting. We sat in a cluster on the outdoor bleachers. Throckmorton stood before us, wearing Purdue athletic shorts that showed off his muscular legs.

"Tuesday is the first official practice, but we might as well get something done, since you're all here." He spoke in a crisp, no-nonsense voice. "Those of you who brought your cleats, we'll get some times on the forty-yard dash." He blew the whistle. "Spread out and start stretching. Don't rush it. I don't want any pulled hamstrings the first day of practice."

I stretched near Derrick, the kid with frosted hair who sat next to me in English.

"Throckmorton played middle linebacker at Purdue," Derrick murmured. "From what I hear, the dude was nasty."

We lined up to get timed for the forty. Throckmorton positioned himself at the starting line, holding a clipboard to record each kid's time. Mr. Dunbar, one of the assistant coaches, stood at the finish line with a stopwatch.

The first kid weighed well over two hundred pounds. He'd be trying out for guard or tackle, I figured. His time was 6.1—not bad for such a big kid. The next boy, who was clearly out of shape, did a lumbering 7.7. Some kids snickered.

"That will not cut it," Throckmorton said sharply. "You gotta do better than that, Trey."

"I will," the poor kid mumbled.

Other times: 5.95; 6.4; 6.6; 7.8; 6.3.

"Rowan Pohi." Throckmorton nodded at me. "C'mon, Ro, let's see what you got."

I stepped up to the starting line and leaned forward.

"Ready, set—go!"

I exploded up the track, reminding myself to keep a short, compact stride, knees tucked under my chest. I sprinted all-out, fixing my eyes ten feet beyond the finish line so I wouldn't be tempted to slow down at the end.

Coach Dunbar stared at his stopwatch. "This can't be right," he muttered. "Four point seven three."

Throckmorton glanced up from his clipboard. "Four seven three?"

Dunbar shrugged. "That's what the watch says."

Throckmorton looked at me. "Sorry, Rowan, but I'm gonna need to see that again. You want to take a break? We can skip you and come back in a few minutes."

"No, I think I'm ready."

I lined up again.

"Ready, set—go!"

I churned my legs, picturing Seth and Brogan as I burst over the finish line.

"Four point nine," Dunbar called.

Throckmorton whistled. "Nice going, Ro."

"Thanks."

"I'm not planning to keep many sophomores on varsity," Throckmorton said. "But if you can catch the ball like you run— well, you've got a shot at one of the wide-receiver positions."

Derrick drifted over. "Four point seven. Yow."

"Decent," I admitted.

Derrick laughed. "Usain Bolt ran a four point three seven in the forty in the Olympics. That's the world record. So, yeah, I'd say a four point seven is more than decent."

My speed in the forty caught the attention of other kids too; I could see them looking over at me. Which felt good. But that good feeling started melting the moment I walked out of White- stone, and it was gone by the time I stepped onto the cross- town bus.

I made hamburger stew for supper. I started by cutting up onions and garlic, using the paring knife that had been Mom's favorite. I remembered her small hands, how fast she worked, almost like a blur as she chopped the garlic cloves into perfect little slices. I could imagine her standing in the kitchen, helping me prepare the food.

Usually making supper calmed me down, but not today. I kept picturing Seth and Brogan, and when I did I could feel tiny tendrils of panic, like icy air bubbles, rising in my gut.

So what if Heather liked Rowan/me? So what if he/I could run the forty-yard dash in four point seven seconds? None of that mattered. Rowan was a sinking ship.

No money for tuition.

No transcript from my previous school.

Seth and Brogan couldn't wait to blow my cover.

Not only that, but I was getting marked absent every day at Riverview High School. Any day now the school secretary would pick up the phone and call my father.

What the hell was I thinking? Why couldn't I have shut my mouth and gone to Riverview with Marcus and Poobs? As I sliced the onions, a stinging odor rose up from the cutting board, making my eyes smart and tear.

What should I do, Mom?

Cody came into the kitchen and looked at me curiously.

"Are you crying, Bobby?"

"It's just the onions," I said. "Set the table."

That night I made a goal for myself to read twenty pages of

To Kill a Mockingbird, but I couldn't get beyond three pages. So I closed that book and picked up *One Flew Over the Cuckoo's Nest.* Twenty minutes later I had finished it. I thought it was a great book, though I didn't know what to think about the ending. It was mixed, sad but also hopeful. A book like that pulls you out of yourself, zaps you into another world.

I was glad to escape my life, even for only a half-hour or so. But the moment I switched off the light, all my problems came flooding back in. I felt that panic again. I couldn't shut it off.

I had no idea what to do. There was no way I would pay Seth any money. Not ten bucks; not even ten cents. That was not an option. Given that fact, and given the evil gleam in Seth's eyes, it was hard to imagine how my Whitestone story could have a happy ending.

TWENTY

Saturday morning my father cooked pancakes. He stood at the stove wearing a T-shirt that said STILL PLAYS WITH CARS. I remembered Mom giving him that shirt for his birthday. We had all laughed, like a happy family; even Cody got the joke.

My father whistled as he flipped the pancakes; he always looked relaxed when he had a day off, which wasn't very often. The radio was playing classic rock, Gregg Allman, "I'm No Angel." Cody sat at the table holding a Spider-Man action figure, wearing two feathers in his hair.

"A two-feather day, huh?" I said. "What's the occasion, Code-ster?"

"I'm going to a birthday party!" he cried. "We're going to Chuck E. Cheese!"

I poured a tall glass of OJ and sat down at the table. "I used to love Chuck E. Cheese when I was a little squirt like you."

He looked indignant. "I'm not a little squirt!"

"Okay, calm down," I told him.

"I got a loose tooth." Opening his mouth, Cody touched one of the fang teeth on top, moving it slightly with his thumb.

"Cool." I nodded. "When it falls out, you might get a visit from the tooth fairy."

"Yeah!"

"Pancakes?" my father offered.

"All right, sure."

"Wanna hear a joke, Bobby?" Cody asked.

Do I have a choice? I thought.

"What's a ghost's favorite kind of pancakes?"

"I dunno. What?"

"Boo-berry!" He let out a huge horse laugh. My brother adored his own jokes. He was forever cracking himself up.

"What are you doing today?" my father asked.

"Going to CarWorks," I told him. "How many oil changes do you have for me?"

"Six."

"Okay, good." I really needed the money.

"Vacuum them cars out real good," he told me. "You should be done by one o'clock, maybe sooner if you hustle."

"Where's the key?"

"On the table." He flipped my pancakes. "Don't lose it. And,

131

Bobby, be real careful when you pull those cars into the garage."

"I've done it before."

"Yeah, but you aren't supposed to drive at all," he reminded me. "If my insurance guy ever found out, he'd have a royal shit fit."

Cody grinned. "Shit fit!"

I swatted Cody on the arm. "Don't say that word!"

"Hey!" He swatted me back.

After breakfast I caught the downtown bus to Fifteenth Street and walked three blocks to Remington, where CarWorks was located. It took several tries before I found the right key and unlocked the door. Inside it was eerily quiet. Mechanics typically don't work on Saturday, and it did feel weird to be working alone in such a large space. But it was nice too. I had worked on Saturdays a few times before, and I could get a lot done when there was nobody else around.

The car keys hung on hooks on a board inside my father's office. When I pressed a button, the large doors began to lift on service bay number 1. The first car was a green Subaru. I got into the car, started it, and drove about fifty feet into the first bay. It wasn't much of a drive, but for me it was a blast because I didn't have a driver's license and wouldn't get one for at least a year. It was surprising that my father let me drive at all. He wasn't the kind of person who looked the other way.

I opened the hood and unscrewed the oil filter cap. Then I climbed into the bay below the Subaru, located the oil pan, and used a wrench to unscrew the drain plug, making sure I had the large plastic bucket in place to catch the old oil. Doing an oil change was a cinch. I often thought that if regular people knew how easy it was, they would all start doing it themselves. (And I'd be out of a job.)

After I got done changing the oil, I vacuumed out the car. CarWorks had an industrial-size vacuum with three times the suction power of an ordinary vacuum, so it was fun to use. Vacuuming was a "value-added service" my father provided for the cars he worked on. I found $1.62 in coins on the floor and between the seats of the Subaru. I always found tons of lost coins when I vacuumed—my all-time record was $4.86. My father had directed me to put all the change in a paper cup and leave it in the cup holder, which is what I did.

"Leaving that cup of coins may seem like a little thing," my father said, "but if it builds the customer's trust, even a little, it's worth it."

I whistled as I worked, happy to have a job that would keep my mind off the train wreck that was my life. Plus I was happy to be making money. I needed to pay back what I'd borrowed from Marcus and Big Poobs. I hated having any debt hanging over me. But before I paid them back, I needed to buy the White-stone blazer.

Later that afternoon I took Cody to the Jamaican festival at People's Park. I thought I smelled ganja, but couldn't be 100 percent sure. A tall guy in dreads was handing out samples of Jamaican Blue Mountain coffee. You could buy all kinds of Jamaican food: jerk chicken, green bananas, even curried goat. There were games, a steel-drum band, and face-painting for the little kids. A chubby clown made a dog out of balloons and gave it to my brother. It was good to see him smile.

Everybody seemed to be in a good mood—except me. I was wound tight inside. I kept seeing the faces of Seth and Brogan. I couldn't get them out of my head.

We were just about to leave when a familiar voice rang out.

"Rowan!"

It was Derrick, the tall kid in my English class who was also trying out for the football team. He was standing by the fence with a group of Whitestone kids. I waved but kept moving.

Cody squinted up quizzically in the afternoon sun.

"Hey, Bobby! He called you Rowan!"

"He's silly," I said, and pulled a glob of blue cotton candy off his chin.

Later that day I decided to text Marcus and Big Poobs.

Meet IHOP?

IL B der, Poobs texted back.

Nothing from Marcus.

At the IHOP four senior citizen types had set up a command post in the booth where we usually sat. Across the room I spotted Big Poobs taking up one entire side of a booth, a bench meant for two. I was really glad to see him. We each ordered root beer and waited in silence until the waitress brought them to the table.

"Power straws?" Poobs suggested uncertainly.

"No." I shook my head. "How's school?"

Poobs groaned. "Riverview is the pits this year. Some kid brought a knife into school—you heard about that, right? The administration freaked. They totally overreacted, installed metal detectors at both entrances. It sucks. Now we have to show up twenty minutes early."

"Or late."

It was Marcus!

"Shove over," he told Poobs, flopping down next to him.

"Hey, Marcus," I said carefully.

"Bobby." Marcus's face was expressionless. "Or is it Rowan? I can't remember which."

"I told you I was sorry."

"It's cool." Marcus picked up the menu. "I'm not pissed off anymore."

"So we're good?" I persisted.

"Good enough." He studied the menu without looking at me. "So. How is life with the Stonys?"

"Great," I said sarcastically. "Couldn't be better."

Marcus looked up from the menu. "What's wrong?"

Sighing, I told them all about Seth and Brogan.

"Seth is going to rat me out unless I pay him," I concluded. "What am I going to do? He's got me by the balls."

"I think I remember that twerp," Marcus said slowly.

"Maybe you should pay them," Poobs suggested.

I lifted one eyebrow. "Maybe you should eat my sweaty jock. I'm not going to pay anyone."

"Then try to talk to him," Poobs said.

I glared at him. "Don't you think I already have?"

"Guys like that don't listen to reason, ever," Marcus put in. "Trust me, I know from experience. What's this moron's name? Seth? We may need to break Seth's face. I'm serious."

"I thought of that," I admitted. "But, c'mon, let's be real. We're not the face-breaking type. We're not face-breakers."

"I could squash him like a bug," Poobs said.

Marcus snorted. "You never hit anybody in your life."

"But I could," Poobs insisted.

Marcus smiled. "But you wouldn't. I hate to tell you, dude. You're a gentle giant, not a fighter."

"Whatever." Big Poobs turned to me. "So what are you going to do?"

"Honestly? I have no idea. Not one." I crunched a big piece of ice between my teeth. "But I'd better come up with something quick. I'm running out of time."

TWENTY-ONE

TWENTY-ONE

ON MONDAY MORNING MY FATHER WAS SIPPING HIS COFFEE, leaning back against the counter, when I came into the kitchen.

"Ready for school?" he asked.

"Yeah," I muttered. He didn't ask which school, so technically it wasn't a lie. Or so I told myself. I had on my jeans plus my ecofriendly USE/LESS T-shirt. I knew that wearing the new khakis and the green Whitestone shirt would prompt questions from my father, questions I wasn't prepared to answer. Over the weekend I had washed my Whitestone uniform and stowed it in my backpack. I had an extra jersey in my school locker.

I downed a bowl of cereal, two jelly doughnuts, and a glass of orange juice, and ran to catch the bus. When I got off, I ducked into the restroom at a nearby McDonald's, got rid of my old threads, transformed myself into Rowan Pohi, and emerged as . . . *Super Stony!*

138

For some fool reason (the sugar from those two jelly dough-nuts?) I felt terrific, which was completely irrational given the reality of my life. How on earth was I going to . . .

- cough up close to fourteen thousand dollars for tuition?
- produce the transcript from Piñon High that Ms. Ryder kept asking for?
- stop Seth and Brogan from revealing my true identity?
- prevent Riverview High from contacting my father about my absences?

Brogan was right: I was royally screwed. My strategy? Stick my head in the sand and refuse to think about it. I was Dr. Denial. A ticking time bomb.

Because of the early release, we followed a shortened schedule that day. In biology, Heather handed me a tightly folded note. It contained spaces to check *yes* or *no*, like on a test.

(1) You're coming to my house at 1, right?
Yes ___ No ___
(2) Did you remember your bathing suit?
Yes ___ No ___
(3) (My mother won't be home till 3:45)

I marked yes, and yes, and smiled in response to number 3 as I handed the note back to her.

When I arrived at *Señor* Backman's class, I found Robin waiting for me. She didn't look happy.

"What's wrong?"

"Remember that necklace I was wearing last week? Well, my English teacher made me take it off. Said there's no jewelry allowed at Whitestone. I couldn't believe it."

I couldn't believe it either, but then I realized I hadn't seen a single kid wearing jewelry.

"I mean, it was a crucifix, for Christ's sake!"

Realizing what she just said, we both burst into laughter.

"Nice one!" I told her.

"Hey, it's early release today," Robin said. "Do you feel like going to the park after school? We could study Spanish or something."

I was intrigued about the *or something* part. "Well, uh, I can't." I tried not to sound guilty. "I'm kind of busy today. Maybe we can do it another time, okay?"

Robin looked like she had expected me to say no.

"No worries," she murmured, and we both ducked into the classroom.

They didn't have regular lunch but I was starving, so I bought a mini-pizza in the dining room. There were plenty of empty tables, so I claimed one and started to eat. I had taken only one bite when I saw them. Seth approached, with Brogan a half a step behind.

"Yo, 'Rowan Pohi.'" It was oh-so-clever the way Seth put air quotes around the name. He sat directly across the table from me. Brogan took the seat to my left, which made me feel surrounded, hemmed in.

"Go sit somewhere else," I told him.

Brogan smiled. "But I want to be close to you."

"If you don't move," I warned, "I'm going to smear pizza sauce all over that nice clean T-shirt. I will do it."

Reluctantly, he got up and moved next to Seth.

"So?" Seth asked. "What will it be, Bobby?"

I didn't see any point in wasting time or playing dumb. "I'm not paying you nothing."

"That's a double negative," Seth observed.

I gave him a level look. "You're damn right it is."

Seth sighed. "Then I guess I'll talk to Dr. LeClerc."

"Why are you messing with my life, you asshole?" Roughly, I pushed back my chair. "I didn't do anything to you."

Seth leaned forward. The acne on his right cheek made a pattern that looked familiar, like one of those star constellations, possibly Cassiopeia.

"Your problem is you really believe you're living in a fairy tale," Seth said quietly. "A once-upon-a-time story. There's a brave knight fighting against all odds. A brave knight wearing a disguise so nobody knows who he really is. That's you. You climbed a magic beanstalk and discovered a whole new magical world. That's Whitestone. There's even a pretty princess with long blond hair, sort of like Goldilocks, only much hotter."

"She has nice, er, hands," Brogan put in, cupping his hands about a foot away from his chest.

"Shut up," I told him.

"But with any fairy tale there's got to be trouble too," Seth continued. "Little Red Riding Hood is just another boring story until the Big Bad Wolf comes along, right? Every story needs a bad guy. That's me. I'm the bad guy."

I blinked at him. "You're mangling your fairy tales."

Seth smirked. He was enjoying himself.

"I'm real good at that. Mangling things. It's my specialty."

"Well, you're wasting your breath," I told him. "I've got nothing to say."

Seth cracked his knuckles. "Me too. I'm done talking. Wednesday at noon is your deadline. You pay me ten bucks by Wednesday at lunch, or I walk into LeClerc's office and tell him the truth. It's real simple. You've got two choices, Bobby Steele. Pay or go away."

I glared at him. "So you'd rat me out."

Seth flashed an evil smile. "In a heartbeat."

I shook my head. "No."

Seth stood and gazed down at me. "Then you're gone."

I had no choice but to try a different direction. With a Herculean effort, I manufactured a sympathetic smile.

"C'mon, Seth, you don't want to do this. Why would you want to get me kicked out of Whitestone? You're better than this. You are."

Seth seemed to find this idea amusing. He glanced over at his friend. "Is he right, Bro? Am I better than this?"

Brogan chuckled. "Nope."

"Rowan?"

Ms. Ryder. The woman was standing in front of the table.

I swallowed. "Yes?"

"Dr. LeClerc would like to see you in his office."

"Me?"

"He said it's important." She noticed my pizza, which I'd barely touched. "Do you want to finish your lunch first?"

"No, that's okay. I'll be right there."

"Ooooh, Bobby's busted!" Brogan murmured as Ms. Ryder walked away.

When I entered his office, Dr. LeClerc stood and motioned to a seat across from his desk. I sank into the leather chair, gripping the padded arms like they were lifelines. I noticed that

Ms. Ryder had stayed in the office, standing at a discreet distance behind me and to the right.

My heart was hammering.

Breathe, I told myself. *Breathe.*

"Do you know why we called you here?" LeClerc asked.

"No."

"Well, we have some news for you, Rowan." The white-haired man gazed at me thoughtfully. Then his face broke into a sudden grin. "You won the writing scholarship!"

I was stunned. "I did?"

LeClerc reached out and grabbed my right hand. "The committee thought the essay you wrote was truly outstanding. We were all impressed by both your command of the language and the depth and passion of your ideas. Congratulations!"

I turned to shake hands with Ms. Ryder, but she surprised me with a big hug.

"This is wonderful, Rowan," she gushed. "I'm thrilled for you!"

"Well, uh, th-thanks," I stammered. "So, but, does that mean—"

LeClerc made a fist and pumped it. "You hit the jackpot, Rowan. A full scholarship to Whitestone."

"Wow." I was flabbergasted.

"There will be some paperwork to fill out," LeClerc added, "but we can take care of that another time."

"Uh, thanks."

I didn't know what more to say, so I kept my mouth shut. I started to leave, but Ms. Ryder lightly touched me on the arm.

"Rowan, this scholarship does change things a bit. I've talked to your teachers and they all report that you're doing very well. Although your Spanish could use a bit of improvement."

"I'm working hard on that," I put in.

She smiled. "I'm sure you are. Anyway, don't sweat the transcripts from your last high school. I'm sure they'll send them eventually. This scholarship proves that you're a keeper at Whitestone. You're here to stay."

TWENTY-TWO

HEATHER SUGGESTED WE WALK TO HER HOUSE. I KEPT MY head down and stepped lively, hoping we wouldn't run into Robin, which would have been *very* awkward. It wasn't until we'd gotten five blocks from Whitestone that I started to relax.

It was one of those beautiful early fall days when there's just a hint of a chill in the air. I kicked an acorn, watched it skitter down the sidewalk and fall through a sewer grate.

"Did you remember to bring your suit?" Heather asked.

"I did."

"Bathing suit or birthday suit?"

"I brought both," I replied without missing a beat.

She grinned. "Well, well, Rowan, don't you just think of everything?"

Heather lived on the Heights in Royal Oaks, a gated community about three-quarters of a mile from Whitestone. She waved at the guard as we entered. The houses were enormous, each mansion bigger than the last, with sweeping lawns and manicured hedges.

"I smell money," I muttered. The first car I spotted was a Mercedes 500. The next one was a silver Jag. "I rest my case."

"It's true," she admitted, "but most of our neighbors are friendly."

"Do you have any brothers or sisters?" I asked.

"My brother, Bastian," she said, fiddling with the lock. "He's in fourth grade. How about you?"

"I've got a brother too. Cody. He's five."

She smiled. "They're cute at five; by ten they start growing devil's horns. Bastian's okay, I guess. He goes to the lower school at Whitestone. Luckily, they don't have early release today."

The first thing I noticed when we stepped through the front door was a tree. A real one. I gazed far up at the branches and the series of skylights beyond.

"That's a tree," I said stupidly.

"It is," she said, like it was no big deal. "A birch tree."

I touched the smooth white bark.

"Yeah, b-but how?" I stammered. "I've never seen a tree growing inside a house."

"My father believes that houses should bring in the natural world—what better way than with a living tree?" she said. "He designed this house himself; it's won a bunch of awards."

Heather gave me a quick tour of the house, which was immense. The ceilings soared twenty feet or higher. There was a gorgeous family room (huge stone fireplace, plush leather couches). Beyond that I noticed another room, smaller and cozier, with a second fireplace and a pretty table made entirely of tinted blue glass. A blue ceramic bowl filled with chocolates sat on top of it.

"What's that room for?"

She shrugged. "I dunno. We aren't supposed to go in there."

"But . . . what about those chocolates? Don't you and your brother ever eat them?"

"It's off-limits. We can't touch it."

I was truly amazed. "Those chocolates wouldn't last long in my house."

The walls in the hallway featured photographs of horses, and Heather stopped to tell me about each one.

"That's Onyx," she said, pointing at a photograph. I'm no horse expert, but I could tell she was a beauty, jet-black with huge soulful eyes. And something else was becoming clear: Heather's family was *very* rich.

"Is that your father?" I asked, pointing to a man standing beside the horse.

"Yeah."

"Is he the horse person in the family?"

She shook her head. "Mom. Dad just sort of went along with it. Then one day he invited his assistant, Maggie, to saddle up. She was twenty-five. And the two of them sort of rode off into the sunset."

"They fell in love?"

"Love, or lust."

"Ouch. Sorry."

"That was four years ago. For a while things were rough around here. Mom had your classic breakdown, but she pulled herself together and now things are okay. Mom and Maggie get along fine now, believe it or not."

Light steam drifted up from the surface of the pool, which was rectangular and tucked behind a thick hedge. The pool area had lots of hanging plants, which made it feel as lush as a garden and very private.

"Swim?" she offered.

"Okay. The water isn't cold, is it?"

"Nope. Mom heats it through the middle of October. You can change in the pool house. I'll grab some towels."

When I emerged, Heather was already standing waist-deep in the water, wearing a black two-piece bathing suit. She looked sensational.

There was a mischievous gleam in her eyes. "Did I tell you that I'm half mermaid and half girl?"

"I don't think you mentioned that."

"Well, I am," she said solemnly.

I dipped my right foot into the water. "Which half is which?"

She grinned provocatively. "Why don't you come in and find out?"

So I jumped in. She moved toward me until we were touching, and the fronts of her feet were resting on mine. Or on Rowan's. Rowan the Romancer! Unbelievable to find myself alone in this fabulous house with a girl like Heather Reardon. To have such treasure just fall into my/Rowan's lap! Marcus and Poobs would never have believed it. I could barely believe it myself.

"I almost didn't recognize you without your school uniform," I teased. "I—"

She shut me up with a kiss.

"Glad we got that out of the way," she murmured.

"I had a dream about kissing you in the planetarium." We were both speaking in low voices, just above a whisper.

"Yeah? Was it as good as this?"

We kissed again. I was aware of a dozen sensations: the silky water, her warm mouth, her arms crossing my spine and pulling me tight against her.

"Almost," I said.

"Almost isn't good enough. Not nearly."

This time I could feel sparks jumping from every point of contact—mouth, chest, belly, thighs, and feet—where her body touched mine.

We stayed in the pool for almost forty-five minutes. As it turned out, we didn't swim a lick that day. Not that it was boring; oh, far from it. And I kept thinking: How could my life be so absurdly wonderful—and so terrible—all at the same time?

On Tuesday afternoon I almost skipped football. Then I realized that this might well be my last practice, so I finally decided to go. Throckmorton met with eight of us who were trying out for wide receiver. For the first half-hour he walked us through the basic pass routes: screen, slant, quick out, deep out, curl, and fly. I could see that making the team would not be automatic; there were three or four other players who were big and rangy. I had a speed advantage, maybe, but would that get me on the team?

"It's not enough to be fast," Throckmorton warned. "To be a good receiver you've got to be elusive too. You have to get separation between yourself and whoever is covering you. *Get separation.* I want you to say those words ten times every night before you fall asleep. *Get separation.* Make that your personal mantra."

It hadn't been a strenuous workout, so that evening I went out for my regular run. While I ran I repeated that phrase: *Get separation.* I must have repeated those words a thousand times. I broke the phrase into four parts to create a nice regular rhythm:

> get separ aaaaa   shun
> bum bum-dee bum bum
> get separ aaaaa   shun
> bum bum-dee bum bum

I ran five miles that night, and then did an extra loop to make it six, trying to exhaust myself so I could sleep. When I had finished, I stopped outside our building, taking a few minutes to cool down and catch my breath before I went inside.

The moment I entered our apartment, something seemed wrong. I detected an ominous odor, a smell both strange and familiar. My heart started banging in my chest. I rushed into the kitchen.

My father.

Holding a hot iron in his right hand.

Cody standing less than two feet away.

My eyes flew open wide.

My father caught the meaning of my look.

Carefully, he put the iron down on the ironing board, where a small white shirt was stretched out.

"What is your problem?" he demanded.

"Nothing," I mumbled.

"Nothing?"

"No." I shook my head.

"Tomorrow's school picture day, and I thought it would be a good idea if somebody ironed your brother's goddamn shirt." He practically bit off each word. "Do you have a problem with that?"

"No."

"*Do* you?" He sounded pissed.

"No."

My brother was leaning against the couch, working a yo-yo. He sent it down and up, down and up, making a whirring sound that broke the silence.

"I'm sorry," I managed.

My father stared. I don't even have words for what I saw in his eyes—something heartbreaking and wounded. Or worse.

Then he blinked; the spell was broken. He went back to ironing Cody's shirt. He did it clumsily, like he had never done it before, which he probably hadn't. My brother stood nearby, working his yo-yo, as silent as my father. I went into the bathroom and turned on the shower.

That night the algebra homework was hard—solving quadratic equations—and I was too upset to concentrate. The strings of numbers and variables seemed pointless. I closed the textbook and shut my eyes. When I did, all I could picture was my father holding that iron in his big hand.

What should I do, Mom?

Okay, so maybe I did overreact. I was still mad at my father. I couldn't help it. Not so much because he'd hurt my mother, but because he'd chased her away from the family. Because he'd made her feel like she had to leave.

Cody wanted a story before bed, so I got up from my desk and went to his bedroom. His white shirt, freshly ironed, hung on his doorknob like a silent rebuke to me. I read him a few chapters from Captain Underpants (always a big favorite), shut off his light, and went back to my room. I could hear the TV in the den, a baseball game.

At ten o'clock I went into the den, determined to make one final attempt to apologize. But the TV had been turned off; Turf was sleeping on the couch. My father had gone to bed, and the door to his room was closed.

TWENTY-THREE

FOR SOME REASON MY FIVE SENSES WERE UNUSUALLY alert on Wednesday morning. From my bedroom, even with the door shut, I could hear Cody in the bathroom humming the Spider-Man song while he brushed his teeth.

I took the bus to school. When I swiped my card and entered Whitestone, I could feel its particular odor wash over me, a smell quite different from Riverview's. Maybe it was the expensive wax they used to polish the floors. Maybe it was the antique wooden bookcases and sculptures breathing out exotic odors from faraway places.

Whap!

Whirling around, I encountered Derrick, who had unloaded on my right arm. It started to throb, but I didn't want to give him the satisfaction of seeing me rub it, so I jabbed him back.

"We get our helmets and pads today," he told me. "There's a full-contact practice after that."

"I'll be ready."

"Friendly warning," Derrick said. "If you go to catch a pass, I will hit you."

"If you can keep up with me," I countered as I headed off in the direction of the sophomore corridor.

I stowed the books I would need for the afternoon in my locker.

"Hi, Rowan." Heather Reardon came over and moved two inches closer to me than was absolutely necessary.

I grinned. "Hey there."

She touched the sleeve of my Whitestone shirt. "I think you look better when you're not wearing this."

"Uh, thanks."

"So how did you like the pool?"

"Great, except for one pesky mermaid I ran into." I closed my locker and spun the dial. "Seriously, Heather, that house of yours is phenomenal."

"I'd love to see yours." She leaned her head against my locker. "Why don't you invite me over sometime?"

I laughed nervously. "There's not much to see. I bet our entire apartment could fit in your family room."

She shrugged. "So what? If it's where you live, then I'm interested."

"Well, I guess so." I couldn't picture Heather there.

Talking with Heather, I felt like I was surrounded by a magical ring of protection, like nothing could harm me. But as the day began, I had to fight off several spasms of dread. I couldn't avoid the fact that this might well be my final day at Whitestone.

Robin was waiting for me outside of Spanish class.

"You smell . . . different," I said.

"I'm wearing a tiny bit of perfume," Robin admitted with a worried expression. "I figured what the heck, you know? It can't hurt. I hope it's not too loud or anything."

"Stop apologizing for yourself," I gently scolded. "It's not too strong. It smells nice."

Señor Backman tried to bring me down in Spanish. He singled me out and peppered me with difficult questions. But I had studied my verbs; I was ready for him. I handled the responses flawlessly, making sure to answer in the same verb tense he used.

¿Usted irá al partido?

Sí, iré al partido.

¿Usted iba a venir?

Sí, iba a venir, I replied.

Señor Backman tested me like this several more times. Finally he gave me a grudging nod of approval and backed off. I could feel Robin smiling from across the room.

I glanced at the clock: 9:45. In two hours and fifteen minutes I would have my showdown with Seth. Would Robin still admire me after that?

Lunchtime/crunch time. The menu featured shepherd's pie, Whitestone chili, and barbecued pulled-pork sandwiches. Tasty options if you were hungry, but I seemed to have lost my appetite. I decided to hit the salad bar and then carried my tray to the corner table.

It wasn't long before Seth strolled over, all loose and casual, with Brogan a step behind. Like Batman with Robin.

"Yo." Seth offered both hands. "Slap me ten, Bobby."

I speared a cherry tomato with my fork and wondered: What would happen if I ignored them completely? Simply pretended they didn't exist?

Seth took the chair directly across from me. He slouched down, resting his forearms on the table.

"Dunno if you heard, but today is Wednesday," he began. "And around here, Wednesday is payday."

"Save it, Seth," I said. "I'm not paying you or anybody else."

"You've had all this time to think about it, and that's the best you could come up with?" Seth looked at me in astonishment.

"Where's your imagination, Bobby? I didn't think you were that stupid."

I stared back at him. "Apparently I am."

Seth sighed. "So you know what's going to happen next. I don't want to do this, but you're not giving me any choice."

As he started to get up, I grabbed the sleeve of his shirt and pulled him down so he was eye level with me.

"Why are you doing this? Why?"

"Why?" Seth carefully removed my hand from his sleeve. He didn't look rattled. In fact, his face was wide-eyed with wonder. "You want me to tell you why?"

"Yeah, why?"

"Because you don't belong here." Seth's expression turned fierce. "You couldn't get into Whitestone like everybody else. Oh, no, not you, Bobby Steele. That's not your way, is it? No, you had to sleaze your way in, didn't you? You think faking the application and putting on that green shirt makes you a Stony? Huh? It's about time you take off your disguise and let everybody know that you're nothing but a fake, a fraud."

Seth and Brogan left, and this time I didn't try to stop them. A little dazed, I watched them walk across the cafeteria.

Later, I went to U.S. history. The teacher, Mrs. Tillett, was young and very easy on the eyes, but today I couldn't pay attention. I closed my eyes. A picture appeared in my mind, an idyllic scene: being with Heather Reardon at her family's farm, riding horses side by side, the two of us following a winding creek that sparkled in the morning sun.

The classroom door opened and Ms. Ryder walked in. Her face looked solemn, like somebody'd just died.

"Excuse the interruption," she said to Mrs. Tillett. "I need Rowan to come with me."

As I stood and gathered my things, I felt a jolt of panic followed by a wave of relief that this whole situation would finally get resolved one way or another.

Ms. Ryder did not speak to me as we went down the hall. I followed her into Dr. LeClerc's office. The headmaster was sitting on a corner of his desk when we walked in. He looked agitated.

"What is your name, young man?" LeClerc demanded.

I hesitated. "Well—"

"It's time to come clean!" he said sharply. He waved several sheets of paper. "You have been representing yourself as Rowan Pohi. That's how you signed your essay. Isn't it?"

"Yes," I said reluctantly.

LeClerc took a half step toward me and folded his arms. I could see the fine network of veins on his cheeks.

"It has come to my attention that in fact your name is Robert Steele. Is that true? Is that who you are?"

"Yeah," I admitted. At that moment I did feel like a fraud. "My name is Bobby Steele."

LeClerc shot an amazed glance at Ms. Ryder, who was standing to his right. Then he turned back to me.

"So, you have been lying from the beginning." LeClerc stared. "Is that what you're telling me?"

"I guess so."

"You *guess* so?" he asked incredulously.

"Yes, sir. I have."

"You are suspended from this school. Immediately." LeClerc jotted a note on a pad of paper. "Tomorrow morning at nine there will be a full hearing of the disciplinary committee. Is that clear, Mr., uh, Steele?"

Almost inaudibly: "Yes."

"What was that?"

I cleared my throat. "Yes, sir. I understand."

"Do not be late. And absolutely do not report to your classes. I will notify your teachers about this situation. Ms. Ryder, please escort Mr. Steele from this building."

Ms. Ryder led me out of the office. We were in the middle of a class period, so the hallways were empty. I was glad not to see Seth, or Brogan, or anybody else I knew.

When she opened the front door, I hesitated. I really liked

Ms. Ryder. She had always been fair with me. I wanted to say something to her, but I didn't know where to start.

"I'm sorry, Ms. Ryder," I managed.

She gave me a searching look. "What in God's name were you thinking? You never went to high school in Arizona, did you?"

"No," I admitted. "But—"

She held up her hand.

"Don't," she said. "You heard what Dr. LeClerc said. I think he was very clear. The disciplinary committee will hold a hearing tomorrow morning at nine. At that time, you will have a chance to say whatever you have to say in your defense."

"What's going to happen to me?"

Ms. Ryder sighed in exasperation, glancing up at the dome ceiling. Then she looked back at me. "If there is anything more important than personal integrity, well, I don't know what it is." Her face was pinched, with upside-down wrinkles on her forehead above each eye. "You have been lying about your identity. That is fundamental. I honestly don't know what the committee will decide, but if it were up to me, you'd be expelled from Whitestone."

TWENTY-FOUR

MY LIFE WAS DISINTEGRATING RIGHT BEFORE MY EYES. BUT I did have a plan, believe it or not, and I tried to convince myself that it might work.

(1) No need to sweat the disciplinary committee meeting because I would not be there. I wasn't going back to Whitestone. Ever.

(2) Tomorrow morning I'd show up at Riverview, take my lumps for missing a bunch of school days (I was prepared for at least a day or two of detention), and climb back into my old life.

(3) Rowan Pohi was history.

(4) My father would never need to know that any of this had happened.

True, there were certain loose ends, such as Coach Throckmorton and the football team. Also Heather Reardon. And, to a

163

lesser extent, Robin Whaley. Plus Derrick, and a few other kids who'd been friendly to me. Hopefully, Heather would be able to see the humor in this mess once I explained it to her. No reason why we couldn't stay in touch, maybe even continue to see each other. There's no law against dating someone who goes to a different high school, right? I texted her twice as I was riding the bus home, but she didn't answer.

Wednesday was spaghetti night and my turn to make supper. I still had no appetite, but my father said the sauce tasted good. Cody liked it too, and why wouldn't he, with the inch of grated cheese he piled on top?

We had almost finished cleaning up the kitchen when the phone rang. My father was closest to the phone, so he answered it. He listened for a long time, saying no more than an occasional "Yes" or "Uh-huh, I see."

He took the phone into his bedroom and closed the door. He was in there so long I started to get a funny feeling in my belly.

"That was Dr. LeClerc," he said when he came out. His face had gone pale. "From Whitestone School."

I swallowed. "Oh."

He blinked. "That's all you can say? Oh?"

Pause.

"Come with me."

We went to the den. Cody wanted to play with his castle guys in front of the TV, but my father told him to take his toys to his room.

We sat on the couch about three feet apart. My father was wearing a blue T-shirt, and I could see fresh cuts on his right forearm. The cuts were evenly spaced, making me think they must have been made by some kind of rotor or chain. There was also a bandage on the knuckles of his right hand where he'd gotten a cut that had needed two stitches. A mechanic's hands and arms really take a beating.

He made a fist with his right hand and gently tapped it against his mouth. "Who is Rowan Pohi?"

I shrugged. "Just a name we invented."

"Who's we?

"Marcus, Big Poobs, and me."

"Spill it, Bobby," he said. "No BS. Tell me everything."

So I told him the whole story. I didn't hold anything back, and it was actually a relief to finally come clean. He listened without interrupting, keeping his eyes fixed on me the whole time.

"Your mother always said Whitestone was a good school," he said thoughtfully. "Is it?"

That surprised me. "Well, yeah. Better than good."

My father lowered his eyes and started chewing on the soft

inside part of his thumb. "LeClerc said there's a disciplinary hearing tomorrow morning. He said you gotta be there at nine."

I looked away. "I'm not going. There's no point. I'm toast. I'm done at Whitestone."

"Done?"

"Yeah."

"Just going to walk away, huh? Drop out?"

"I'll go to Riverview," I added lamely.

"Riverview, huh?" I watched his expression shift gears and slip into angry. "I guess you got it all figured out, don't you? Be whoever you want to be. Take whatever name you want. Show up at whatever school you want."

"I guess I didn't think it all the way through."

He stood up, suddenly restless. I watched him go to the window, crack the blinds, and stare at the street.

"Don't want to be Bobby Steele anymore?" He turned to look at me. "You ashamed of the name? Huh? Is that why you changed it?"

I said nothing, and my nothing said everything.

There was a long pause. Finally, he spoke in a half whisper.

"Maybe if you don't want to call yourself Bobby Steele, well, maybe you don't want to be my son."

"Yes, I do," I said, though I don't know if I said that because it was true or because I knew it was what I was supposed to say.

I saw him working his jaw. Then he peered at me in a peculiar way.

"I guess you're on your own now, Bobby. Good luck."

I blinked. "What do you mean?"

He shrugged.

"You kicking me out?" I asked.

"No. You've got your bedroom. Food in the fridge. A place to live." He closed the blinds. "But you just living here doesn't make us family, neither."

He went to the front door and opened it.

"Where you going?"

"Out."

"AA meeting?" I asked.

But he didn't answer as he strode out the door.

Even though it was raining, I really wanted to go out for a run. But I couldn't leave Cody alone in the apartment, so I stayed. And maybe it's fortunate that I did. If I had gone for a run I might have just kept going, like Mom did, and I might not have come back.

It was a long night. My teachers had assigned a boatload of homework, especially Nardone in English, and I almost started working on it out of habit until I remembered that I was done at Whitestone. I'd never see those teachers again.

I read Cody two books before he went to bed. After that I didn't know what to do with myself.

I retexted Heather. Still no answer.

I turned on the baseball game, but the rain had halted play in the seventh inning. I love baseball, but there is nothing on planet Earth more boring than a ball game during rain delay. I channel-surfed but couldn't find anything worth a damn. When I finally climbed into bed, my father still hadn't come home.

Get separation.

About a year ago Mom had separated herself from me and Cody. After tonight's conversation, I felt emotionally separated from my father too. I felt cut off, detached, separated from my old friends and my new friends both.

Separation? Separation was just about all I had.

I made a pledge myself: I would stop lying. I was sick of it. From now on, no matter what, I was going to tell the truth.

TWENTY-FIVE

TWENTY-FIVE

I TRIED TO TUNE OUT CODY'S JABBERING AT BREAKFAST. My father leaned against the counter, dressed in jeans and a denim work shirt. He sipped his coffee, deep in thought.

Just going to walk away, huh?

I left the house intending to go to Riverview. But when I stepped onto the sidewalk, my feet hesitated, wouldn't move.

What the . . . ?

Opposite Day.

Instead of going toward Riverview, I found myself striding in the direction of the crosstown bus. I was going to Whitestone after all. I let out a string of curses but kept on walking.

On the bus, two girls sat near me, identical twins, bopping to a song on an iPod. They shared earphones and waggled their heads in rhythm. It was kind of eerie how perfectly in sync they were with each other. Even in my miserable state, I couldn't help but smile.

At the school entrance I swiped Rowan's ID card. Surprisingly, it still worked. The door clicked, allowing me to push through. The halls were empty, so I made a beeline for my locker.

On the bus, I had tried to decide whether or not I should wear my uniform to the disciplinary meeting. Wearing it had seemed like a stupid idea. But now that I was inside the school, I knew I had to. I changed right in the empty hallway, peeling off the button-down shirt I was wearing and pulling on the green Whitestone jersey.

Just as I started walking toward LeClerc's office, the bell rang. The hallway flooded with students. I was relieved not to see any familiar faces. I sped down the hallway, trying to be invisible, until Heather stepped in front of me and forced me to stop.

She folded her arms. "Do you mind telling me what is going on?"

I shifted my feet. "What do you mean?"

"Seth told me you're not Rowan."

"I'm not," I admitted.

She stared in disbelief. "So who are you?"

"Bobby Steele." I tried to say it proudly.

She looked like a girl whose worst fears have just been confirmed. "Seth said your father—"

I was done lying. "Yep."

She just stared. Her face had gone to stone.

I glanced at my watch. "Listen, I've got to go to this disciplinary thing, and I can't be late. There's a bunch of stuff I need to tell you. Can we talk later?"

"I don't know." She held her body rigid as she walked away.

"Heather!" I called, but she had already disappeared around the corner.

When I walked into Dr. LeClerc's office, four people sat staring at me from the other side of the table: LeClerc, Ms. Ryder, plus a man and a woman I didn't recognize.

"Sit down, Bobby," LeClerc said, motioning me to an empty seat. His tie featured dozens of tiny tennis rackets in all different colors. "You already know Ms. Ryder. This is Mr. Nylander, who is head of our guidance department. And this is Dr. Horn, dean of student affairs."

Nylander nodded; Dr. Horn offered a weak smile.

Relax, Bobby, I told myself. *You've got nothing to lose because you've already lost everything.* No reason to feel nervous, so why did I? My throat was parched. There was a pitcher of water on the table; I poured myself a glass and quickly drained it.

"This meeting of the Whitestone disciplinary committee is now in session," Dr. LeClerc said curtly. "This committee only convenes when a serious issue arises, one that demands our immediate attention. Your situation certainly meets that standard, Bobby. For nearly a hundred years, the motto at Whitestone has been Achievement and—"

The door opened and a man entered, causing everyone to look over. At first, I didn't recognize him. He was freshly shaved, his hair slicked back, and he was wearing a blue suit jacket that was too small for him.

My father.

"I'm Bob Steele."

I was flabbergasted.

"I'm sorry, but this is a closed meeting," LeClerc told him.

"Not to me it isn't." He shut the door behind him and pointed at me. "I'm Bobby's father. He's a minor, and I've got a right to be here."

LeClerc looked uncomfortable. He glanced at the other members of the committee.

"Very well, then, please have a seat, Mr. Steele. But I would ask you to remain silent while this committee deliberates."

"Fine by me."

He took the seat next to me and gave me a quick nod, which I did not return. With his bad grammar, my father could only make things worse for me. I really didn't want him there.

"Achievement and Integrity," Dr. LeClerc began again. "That

is our motto here at Whitestone Preparatory School, and it is more than just a pretty slogan to put on our stationery. It is a motto we live by. We take it very seriously. Now, the basic facts in this case are not in dispute. It seems quite clear, Bobby, that you have violated the second principle: integrity. You deliberately misrepresented yourself by pretending to be someone else, both on your application and during your brief time here at White-stone. Isn't that true?"

I didn't trust myself to speak but I managed a half nod.

"We are talking about identity theft," Mr. Nylander put in. "That's a very serious thing. If—"

"He didn't steal anybody's identity," my father interrupted. "He made up a new one."

Even though I was alarmed to have my father interrupt the proceedings, I realized he did have a point.

"Mr. Steele," LeClerc warned.

"There's a big difference," my father insisted.

Impatiently, LeClerc drummed the table. "Mr. Steele, you will have your turn to speak. But if you cannot remain quiet and let this committee do its work, I will have to insist that you leave this room. Is that clear?"

My father lowered his eyes. "All right."

"I have a question for you, Bobby," Dr. Horn said. Her short, severe haircut contrasted with her kind face. "Why did you do it? Why did you change your name?"

"I, uh, well, I don't know," I stammered. "At first it was a crazy idea we had, me and a few friends, sort of fun, you know, just goofing around, seeing if we could pull it off. We weren't trying to hurt anyone. But then . . ."

My voice trailed off.

"The prank took on a life of its own," Dr. Horn said, finishing for me.

I nodded. "Yes."

"You must have realized that eventually we would find out," Ms. Ryder said, fingering a sheet of paper. "What about this letter of recommendation? Is Mr. Ramón García a real person?"

"We made him up too," I admitted.

"*You* wrote that letter?" LeClerc demanded.

"A friend did."

"Who?" my father demanded.

"I'd rather not say." I couldn't see any reason to throw Marcus under the bus. "It doesn't matter."

Mr. Nylander cleared his throat. "Where did you come up with the last name Pohi?"

I started to lie, but then I remembered the vow I'd made to myself.

"It's IHOP backwards. International House of Pancakes."

As I suspected, Dr. LeClerc did not have much of a sense of humor. "So, you were trying to make fools out of us, is that it?"

I shook my head without looking at him. "I swear, it was like she said"—pointing at Dr. Horn—"just a harmless prank, Dr. LeClerc. We never really thought Rowan would get accepted. After he did, I got the idea to, you know . . . become Rowan Pohi and come to Whitestone as him."

LeClerc shuffled some papers. I closed my eyes. For some peculiar reason, the image that appeared in my head was that off-limits room I'd seen at Heather's house. The forbidden bowl of chocolates. I should never have set foot in Whitestone. Seth was right: I didn't belong here. I opened my eyes.

Leaning back, Dr. LeClerc sighed. "Look, Bobby, you are not giving us much to go on. This is the time to speak up for yourself. Can you tell this committee why you shouldn't be dismissed from Whitestone?"

I didn't answer because my mind had gone blank. I honestly couldn't think of one good reason.

"Well, I guess that's about it, then," Nylander said.

"Hold it," my father objected. "You said I could have a turn."

"Very well, Mr. Steele," Dr. LeClerc said wearily. "Go ahead."

I closed my eyes, dreading what my father would say or do next.

My father leaned forward, putting his hands on the table. I

175

was sorely aware that they were hands unlike any others in that room. Dark-stained. Muscular. Dangerous. I didn't like to see him displaying those hands, especially with the jagged stitches across his knuckles. They reinforced the idea that he didn't belong in this school. And neither did I.

"I'm not an educated man. Never did the college thing. I work with these." He held up both hands as evidence. "I own CarWorks, an auto-repair shop on Fifteenth and Remington. If we ever worked on your car at my garage, well, I hope we didn't gouge you too bad."

I winced. This clumsy attempt at humor fell flat, as I knew it would.

"I had no idea Bobby was going to Whitestone Prep," he continued. "I figured he was going to Riverview, like he did last year. Why wouldn't I? Bobby has never given me any trouble, so I had no idea there was anything fishy going on until you called me last night. After I got off the phone, me and Bobby had a talk. I told him I was mighty mad about it. Am. That's between us."

He shifted in his chair.

"This kid's in trouble for pretending to be someone else, am I right? The question is—why'd he change his name like that?" He looked at me. "He won't say why, but I think it's partly because his name is my name."

He paused and I was thinking, *Oh God, no, don't . . .*

"Last year me and my wife . . . let's just say things turned ugly between us. Real ugly. I got arrested. My name was in the paper. Maybe you heard about it. Iron Steele. That's me."

Pause.

"Please get to your point, Mr. Steele," LeClerc said carefully.

"I paid for what I did." My father lowered his voice. "I spent more than two months in jail. I felt shame, a boatload of it, and still do. I lost my wife forever. That's my cross to bear. But there's no reason why *this* Bobby Steele"—he pointed at me—"should be punished for what I did. Alls he wanted was a fresh start. Believe me, there's worse things in this world."

He made a fist with his right hand and tapped it lightly against his mouth.

"I'm not saying what my son did was right. It was flat-out wrong, and Bobby knows it. But he's doing good in his classes, isn't he? Didn't he win some kind of scholarship for his writing?"

LeClerc nodded. "That's true."

"All right, then," my father concluded. "Maybe Bobby didn't get into this school the right way, but that don't mean he don't belong."

I closed my eyes, cringing at the way he had mangled that sentence. I prayed that he was finished; fortunately, he was.

LeClerc tapped his pen on the table. "Thank you, Mr. Steele. Your comments are helpful. But I must state for the record that there's a reason we ask students—*all* students—to go through proper admission procedures. We want to make absolutely sure they belong here at Whitestone. It's not just for us; it's for their benefit too. Not every student flourishes in this kind of intense academic environment."

My father looked troubled. "What are you saying?"

"I'm just saying it may well be that Whitestone isn't the right school for Bobby."

"Wait a sec," my father objected. Until now his tone had been mostly congenial, but now I could see dark storm clouds gathering. His voice turned hard.

"His old school, Riverview, got a substandard rating from the state," he said. "Substandard. That's the school he'd have to go back to. So don't try to tell me it would be better for Bobby to leave Whitestone and go back to Riverview. I wasn't born yesterday."

"Mr. Steele, please don't raise your voice," LeClerc warned. "Calm down."

"I spent three years in Mississippi when I was in the navy," my father shot back. "They have a saying down south: 'Don't piss on my back and tell me it's raining.' "

Well, that shut everybody up.

"I think we get your point, Mr. Steele," LeClerc finally said. He pushed back his chair and stood. "Thank you for your perspective. Bobby, I'm going to ask that you and your father please step outside while the committee deliberates."

TWENTY-SIX

DR. LECLERC'S SECRETARY GOT MY FATHER A CUP OF COFFEE.
He thanked her and took a seat on the couch; I sat at the other end. At first there had seemed to be some insane logic in returning to Whitestone, but now it felt like a colossal mistake. It was barely nine thirty, but already I was exhausted. I swear I could have crawled back into bed and slept for a solid month.

"This is one fancy school," my father said, looking around. "You see all that marble in the foyer? That stuff don't come cheap."

"No, it doesn't," I replied, correcting him like I always did, not that it ever made any difference.

I knew I should thank him for coming to support me, but I couldn't bring myself to do it. It felt wrong having him at Whitestone. He just didn't fit in this world.

"Don't you have to go to work?" I asked.

"That's one of the perks of owning your own business. If you want to take the morning off, you can." My father sipped his coffee. "So, I wasn't just talking trash in there, was I? This school is a big upgrade from Riverview."

"Yeah, they've pretty much got everything here," I told him. "There's an Olympic-size pool, a rifle range, even a planetarium, brand new."

"No kidding. What about the teachers?"

"Real good."

"You gonna do any sports?"

"I'm trying out for football. Was."

I got a sudden image of Coach Throckmorton that made me jump up and start pacing.

My father stared. "You okay?"

"What's the point of just sitting here waiting around?" I fumed. "I want to leave."

"Sit down, Bobby," he said calmly. "It would be stupid to leave now. We gave it our best shot in there. Now let's see how this all plays out."

Hearing him use the word *we* irritated me something fierce.

Right then my cell phone buzzed. A text message from Marcus.

Hey puke-head Y arnt U in school?

I texted back: Cant talk TTYL.

I shut off my phone and stowed it in my backpack.

"You won a scholarship, huh?" he said. "I guess you inherited your mother's brains."

"I guess." It was unusual, his asking all these questions about me. And somehow it didn't seem right for him to mention her.

He placed his coffee on the table next to him. Then he leaned forward, resting his forearms on his knees.

"Thirteen months. Since your mother left. I miss her."

I was stressed out, so I wasn't feeling sympathetic. "You make it sound like she just bailed. Just waltzed off."

He raised his eyebrows. "What are you trying to say?"

"Nothing," I mumbled. "Forget it."

"No," he persisted. "C'mon, Bobby. Spill it."

The way he was looking at me, I decided to take a chance.

"She didn't just leave," I reminded him. "You drove her away."

There. I said what I'd never said before. I worried he might try to grab me with those dangerous hands, but at the same time it was a relief to finally get that out in the open.

He didn't go ballistic. Instead, he met my eyes.

"Maybe I did drive her away. Yeah, okay. I did. Would you

believe that every single night of my life I lie in bed wishing I could have a do-over? So I could undo what I done?"

I didn't answer.

"It wasn't just what happened that night either. There was plenty of other times I didn't treat her right."

He was talking to me now, something he hardly ever did. Neither one of us knew how to do it, not with each other.

"I'm sorry, Bobby."

My throat was tight. I could feel him reaching out to me.

"I know."

"That's water under the bridge," he said.

Cold, dark water, I thought, though I conceded his point.

"You told Dr. LeClerc you lost her forever," I said. "But Mom could still come back. I mean, it's technically possible."

He exhaled. "I got the divorce papers six days ago."

I was stunned. "Mom contacted you?"

"Her lawyer did."

"Do you know where she is?"

He shook his head. "Nope. And she don't want me to know."

I took a few moments to try to digest all that.

"What are you going to do about the divorce papers?" I finally asked.

He rubbed his face, which looked crumpled and beaten. "I already signed them and sent them back."

We were quiet for almost a minute. For the first time I understood that Cody and I weren't the only ones who'd lost someone important.

"That suit looks tight," I said, to break the silence.

He unbuttoned the top button on his shirt. "I can't wait to get it off. When I die, whatever you do, don't let 'em bury me in a suit and tie. Okay? I want to be comfortable in my coffin."

"Okay."

"Promise?"

I nodded. For some reason, I almost felt like crying.

Mom wasn't here when I really needed her. But he was. My father showed up. To defend me. I felt an unexpected surge of gratitude.

"Thanks, Dad."

He looked at me warily. "For what?"

"For coming here. For speaking up for me."

He swallowed. "Welcome."

We could hear the sound of voices inside LeClerc's office, though it was impossible to make out any words.

"They're going to expel me."

"They might do that," he said casually. "But that might not be their smartest move, because if they do, I will sue the ass off this fancy school."

"You will not."

"Oh, yes, I will. I'm a fighter, Bobby. I may go down, but I always go down swinging."

I thought about what he had said in LeClerc's office: *Don't piss on my back and tell me it's raining.* That line was an instant classic in my book. I couldn't wait to share it with Marcus and Big Poobs.

The office door opened, and LeClerc appeared.

"You can come in, Bobby. Mr. Steele."

I followed him inside and went to the table. Four people gazed up at us, poker-faced, every one of them. This time I realized I was glad to have my father standing beside me so I didn't have to face the committee alone.

"Your ID card." Dr. LeClerc held out his hand, palm up. "Please surrender it to me."

My heart plummeted at that word: *surrender.*

I pulled Rowan's card from my wallet and handed it to him. LeClerc dropped it into the trash.

"You're going to need a new ID card, Bobby."

Smiles suddenly broke out everywhere. Even my father was grinning. I was the only one who had a case of the stupids. I wouldn't allow myself to believe what was happening.

"What you did was wrong, and very serious," Dr. LeClerc declared formally. "But under the circumstances, looking at the bigger picture, this committee has decided not to expel or punish you. Welcome back, Bobby. You've got yourself a fresh start."

He shook my hand, and my father's too.

"Thanks." I didn't know what else to say.

"You can get a new ID during lunch period," Ms. Ryder said. "And if you hurry, you should be able to make your third-period class."

"I expect that you will let your teachers know your real name," Dr. LeClerc said gently, putting his hand on my shoulder. "If they have any questions, they can contact me."

I turned to my father, but he was waving as he hurried out the door.

Still dazed, I floated down the hall in the general direction of biology. My first selfish thought: I couldn't wait to run into Seth and Brogan.

I ran into Heather instead. Our eyes met, so she couldn't pretend she hadn't seen me.

"Hey," I said.

"So what happened?"

"I didn't get expelled. They're letting me stay." Try as I might, I couldn't suppress a huge grin. "They didn't even punish me."

"Congratulations." But there wasn't a sliver of warmth in her voice. "I've got to get to class."

"Wait!" I said.

She froze. I moved a step closer and put my hand on her arm. It was one of those awkward situations that Rowan Pohi would have known how to handle. But Rowan was gone; I was on my own.

"Listen, Heather, I'm real sorry about this. I know I deceived you, but I swear I'll never do that again. Could I have, like, a do-over?"

She looked at me like I was crazy. "A do-over?"

I nodded and smiled. "I have this fantasy that I could walk up to you and introduce myself: 'Hi, I'm Bobby Steele.' And we could start over again."

Her blue eyes were beautiful but cold.

"That's why they call it a fantasy. Because it doesn't happen that way in real life."

"C'mon, Heather, I'm still the same guy you hung out with in your pool, aren't I?" Sheepishly, I smiled. "I'm throwing myself on the mercy of the court."

Trying to make a joke of it, I knelt down in front of her.

"Get up." She wasn't amused, so I stood up.

"You know what you are?" she said slowly. "You are like one of those bugs that imitate other bugs we studied in science. You snuck into this school by wearing a disguise. You acted like us.

You dressed like us. You pretended you were one of us. But you were never one of us. Never."

"It's way more complicated than that," I told her, but she had already walked away.

TWENTY-SEVEN

I WAS LOOKING FOR ROBIN. INSTEAD I RAN INTO SETH, standing in front of his locker.

"Did you get expelled?" he asked eagerly.

"Change of plans!" I spread my arms wide, feigning disbelief. "Believe it or not, they decided to let me stay. What's up with that, Seth?"

Seth's smile died. "Bullshit."

"Word," I told him. "You can take it to the bank, Seth. I'm not even getting punished. Put that in your pipe and smoke it."

Seth's face looked pained, like I'd just struck him.

"This isn't over," he warned.

"Yes, it is." I took a step toward him. "I haven't told LeClerc that you guys were trying to blackmail me. Yet. I'll keep quiet about it, so long as you leave me alone."

I put my hand on Seth's shoulder; he violently shook it off. I could feel him staring as I walked away, whistling "Zip-a-Dee-Doo-Dah."

By the time I found Robin, I felt like I was punch-drunk, emotionally exhausted. But today was a reckoning day. I needed to talk to her.

"What's all the commotion?" she asked.

"I'm not Rowan Pohi," I blurted out. "I'm Bobby Steele. Seriously."

"But, when, you said . . . How?"

"It's way too long and complicated for me to explain now."

She folded her arms. "Okay, I'll take the condensed version."

I took a deep breath. "See, my friends and I created an imaginary kid. We filled out an application, faked a letter of recommendation, and got him accepted to Whitestone. Then I pretended to be him."

She nodded, like that sort of thing happens every day. "Oh."

"Someone squealed on me, and I almost got expelled," I added. "There's a lot more, but I'd need a couple hours to explain it to you."

"You're serious, aren't you?"

"Yeah."

"So your name is . . . ?"

"Bobby Steele."

"Bobby." She said the name slowly, trying it out on her tongue.

"Do you hate me, Robin?"

She shook her head. "I thought you were interesting the first time I met you, and you're even more interesting now." She paused. "But I do feel kind of sad about one thing."

"What?"

"I'll never talk to Rowan again." She blinked. "I liked that kid."

For the second time it hit me that Rowan Pohi had really and truly gone out of existence.

"Rowan was cute too," she added. "That boy was baberrific!"

"That isn't a word!"

"Listen to you!" She sounded indignant. "You invent a whole new person and you're giving me a hard time for making up a puny little word?"

I laughed, feeling grateful that at least one kid at White-stone was going to accept me as Bobby Steele.

I found Throckmorton sitting at his desk in his office. He froze when I told him. He started to speak, then seemed to change his mind.

"Well, I guess you must have had your reasons for doing what you did."

"I did."

He regarded me thoughtfully. "Can I still call you Ro? As a nickname?"

I shrugged. "Fine with me."

"Go see the trainer, Ro," he told me. "He'll fit you for a helmet and pads. We're doing full-contact drills today."

Later that afternoon, after practice, I met Marcus and Poobs at the IHOP and told them I would buy the sundaes.

"How come you're treating?" Marcus wanted to know. I told them what had happened that day, and they leaned forward, hanging on every word. When I finished, they laughed in amazement. Then we traded high-fives all around.

"So Big Bobby came through," Marcus said with grudging admiration. "When it was crunch time, he had your back."

"Yeah."

"You dodged a major bullet, dude," Poobs put in. "And now you're officially a Stony."

I scooped up the last puddle of hot fudge. "I hope I don't turn into a snotty preppy."

"Not an option," Marcus assured me. "We're going to bust on you just like before."

"I do feel bad about a couple of things."

"What?"

I shrugged. "I don't know. It doesn't seem right. I'm going to Whitestone, and you guys are still going to Riverview."

"Who says life is fair?" Marcus replied.

"Thing is, it didn't have to be me who went to Whitestone. It could have been either one of you."

"No, it couldn't," Marcus replied emphatically. "There was no way in hell I was going to walk into that school."

"Me neither," Poobs put in.

"Don't kid yourself, Bobby," Marcus said. "You were the one. It had to be you. And you'd be an idiot to feel bad about it."

TWENTY-EIGHT

TWENTY-EIGHT

THAT NIGHT DAD GRILLED SIRLOIN STEAKS. WHEN THE three of us sat down to eat, I noticed that something was different.

"Where's your Indian feather?" I asked Cody.

Dad and I stared. Cody's feather was gone.

My brother shrugged. "Being Spider-Man is way cooler than being a Indian."

My father put down his fork. "Spider-Man? So you're not an Indian anymore?"

"Nope." Cody put a chunk of steak into his mouth and started to chew. I glanced over at my father, who raised his eyebrows but said nothing more. I was thinking of that expensive Indian necklace I'd gone back and bought at Kopsky's. When I surprised Cody with it, he was totally blown away, almost knocked me over with a hug. Good thing I gave it to him before his Indian phase wore off.

"I used to wear Spider-Man pajamas when I was in second grade," I said. "Remember, Dad?"

He smiled. "Sure I remember."

Cody almost choked with excitement. "You did? Can I wear them, Bobby?"

"I think Mom packed them away in my closet," I told him. "I'll look for them after supper."

For months and months I'd been obsessing about my mother. I constructed elaborate and detailed scenes in my head, exciting adventures where I would search and finally find her in some distant city. We would fall into each other's arms in a tearful reunion. *Bobby, Bobby, if you only knew how much I missed you and Cody . . .*

I knew now that those were pipe dreams, fantasies. *That's why they call it a fantasy,* Heather told me. *Because it doesn't happen that way in real life.*

I was only beginning to realize how angry I was at Mom for leaving us like that. I had cast Dad as the bad guy and Mom as the innocent victim, but it wasn't that simple. She was the one who walked out on us. But she was paying a huge price for it. She was missing all the important stuff from Cody's life: loose teeth, dumb jokes, birthday parties at Chuck E. Cheese, the zany finger-paintings he did in kindergarten. She'd miss my first football game against Phillips Exeter. She was missing everything.

Still, some things are so real, so vivid, they can't easily be erased from memory. Like Mom's hermit cookies, just out of the oven. I can still taste them. I can still see the dreamy look she got stirring her morning coffee. Those little things, and a million others, make it hard to face the truth.

Goodbye, Mom.

Then there's Heather. I doubt I'll ever forget that afternoon we spent in her pool. For nearly an hour I had the whole world in my hand—two lush planets actually, or binary stars—but that world is gone. I will never get back in that pool with her or touch the trunk of that indoor tree. I will never get to ride Onyx down a wooded trail. Heather had cut me loose. Early release. I could still see the final, closed look on her face, like a deserted beach house before a hurricane with every door and window boarded up.

Goodbye, Heather.

Robin Whaley was surprisingly sympathetic when I told her about it later. We sat outside on the stadium stairs, watching the cheerleaders practice.

"I'm real sorry she broke up with you, Bobby. Really, I am. It's her loss."

"Apparently not," I said with a wry smile.

"Well, you've still got me," Robin murmured after a moment. "Unfortunately, I don't have legs up to my eyeballs like Heather."

"Overrated," I told her.

She smiled. "No, it's not. But thanks for saying that."

When she turned to look up at me, I noticed the pretty sparkle in her eyes.

"There's a film festival at Whitestone this Saturday," she said.

"I already have tickets," I said.

Her eyes narrowed. "Oh, okay."

I pulled two tickets out of my wallet and showed them to her. "One for me, and one for you."

"Oh." She tried to play it cool but couldn't suppress a big grin.

Things got back on track at Whitestone, though I had to spend a lot of time explaining to teachers, coaches, and other kids who I really was. In grade school I once had a friend named Jake Goodwin whose mother remarried. All of a sudden his name changed to Jake Baver. That was weird enough, but at Whitestone my entire name changed. I had to bid farewell to someone who had been with me his whole life.

Goodbye, Rowan.

But not entirely. Once in a while teachers and kids still called me Rowan. Old habits are hard to break; I still answered to that name.

And maybe some of Rowan's confidence—his chutzpah—

had rubbed off on me. Case in point: That girl Robin and I observed from the library conference room, the goddess with red hair, transferred into our English class. She sat right behind Derrick.

"I'm Bronwyn," she said, flashing me a dazzling smile.

In the old days it would have been terrifying to be talking up close and personal to a hottie like that. But now I calmly smiled back at her.

"Nice to meet you. I'm Bobby."

A week later Nardone passed back the essays we'd written on *To Kill a Mockingbird.* I got an A-minus. Bronwyn got a C-minus.

"Writing is not my thing," she whispered when she saw me glance over at her. "I plan it out, but every time my sentences get all knotted up. I wish somebody could help me untangle them."

She looked at me hopefully.

I saw the opportunity but decided to let it pass. "You should check out the writing center. They're open every day after school."

"Oh, okay," Bronwyn said.

I knew I was doing the right thing; still, I mentally sighed, seeing the disappointment in her eyes.

So all in all, my life is solid. I climbed back into my old name— *Hello, Bobby*—and I really like who I am, for the most part. I have a job, friends at two different schools, and a little brother who needs me. Throckmorton says I've got a decent chance of making varsity as a wide receiver. I'm focused. Gradewise, I intend to kick some serious butt at Whitestone. I went to the guidance department and met with Mr. Nylander. He said if I do well at Whitestone I have a great shot at getting accepted to a good college.

As for Dad and me, well, things aren't always perfect, but we know how to make it work. He's been extra busy lately. With the bad economy, people are hanging on to their old cars longer, so business has never been better at his garage. I'm trying to cut him a little slack, to stop mentally correcting him when his grammar gets messed up. He is who he is.

I think about Rowan Pohi more often than you might expect. He was kind of like an imaginary friend, but he was also more than that, much more. He will always have a special place in my heart. Some nights while I'm running or in the moments before I fall asleep, I laugh out loud when I think of the stunts he pulled, walking into Whitestone on a wing and a prayer and a fake ID. That kid had balls. I guess we both did.

I'm grateful to Rowan. I really am. I couldn't have done it without him.